THE DAUGHTERS
OF THE NIGHT

By one of the most prolific writers of the 1920s...

Jim Bartholomew is the young manager of a branch of the South Devon Farmers' Bank, with a love of hunting and horses, and a dislike of routine. What does he have in common with Margot, the beautiful Mrs Markham and a handsome American – and what do the Daughters of the Night, the three Roman deities who brought punishment to evil-doers, have to do with this tale?

THE DAUGHTERS OF THE NIGHT

The Daughters Of The Night

by

Edgar Wallace

Dales Large Print Books
Long Preston, North Yorkshire,
BD23 4ND, England.

British Library Cataloguing in Publication Data.

Wallace, Edgar
     The daughters of the night.

     A catalogue record of this book is
     available from the British Library

     ISBN   978-1-84262-542-2 pbk

Cover illustration © Anthony Monaghan

Published in Large Print 2007

Dales Large Print is an imprint of Library Magna Books Ltd.

Printed and bound in Great Britain by
T.J. (International) Ltd., Cornwall, PL28 8RW

1

Jim Bartholomew, booted and spurred and impatient to be gone, sat on the edge of the table and watched the clock with a sigh. He looked too young a man to be the manager of the most important branch of the South Devon Farmers' Bank, and possibly the fact that his father had been managing director of that corporation before he died had something to do with his appointment.

But those who saw in him only a well dressed young man with a taste for good horses, and imagined that his accomplishments began and ended with riding to hounds or leading a hunt club cotillion, had reason to reverse their judgment when they sat on the other side of his table and talked business.

He glanced at his watch and groaned.

There was really no reason why he should remain until the closing hour, for yesterday had been Moorford's market day and the cash balance had gone off that morning by train to Exeter.

But, if the truth be told, Bartholomew lived in some awe of his assistant manager. That gentleman at once amused and irritated him, and whilst he admired the conscientiousness of Stephen Sanderson there were moments when his rigid adherence to the letter of banking regulations and local routine annoyed Jim Bartholomew unreasonably. He took another look at his watch, picked up his riding whip from the table, and passed into the assistant manager's room.

Stephen Sanderson did just what Jim expected. He looked up at his manager and from the manager to the loud-ticking clock above the door.

'In two minutes we shall be closed, Mr Bartholomew,' he said primly and managed to colour that simple statement of fact with just a tinge of disapproval.

He was a man of forty-two, hard-working and efficient, and Jim Bartholomew's appointment to the management of the Moorford branch had shattered one of the two ambitions of his life. He had no particular reason to love his manager. Bartholomew was an out-of-door man, one who had distinguished himself in the war, who loved exercise and something of the frivolity of life. Sanderson was a student, an indefatigable hunter of references, and found his chief pleasure within the restricted area which a reading lamp throws. Moreover he had a weakness, and this Jim Bartholomew, with his queer inquisitiveness, had discovered, to Stephen Sanderson's embarrassment.

'The vaults are closed, Mr Sanderson,' said Jim, with a smile. 'I don't think two minutes will make a great deal of difference one way or the other.'

Mr Sanderson sniffed, without raising his eyes from the paper upon which he was writing.

'How go the criminal investigations?' asked Jim humorously, and the man flushed and laid down his pen viciously.

'Let me tell you, Mr Bartholomew,' he said hotly, 'that you are making fun of a quality of mine which may one day serve the bank and its interests very well.'

'I am sure it will,' said Jim soothingly, half ashamed of the provocation he had given.

'I have recently had from New York, from a corresponding friend of mine, the threads of a remarkable case,' went on the ruffled Sanderson, taking up an envelope. 'Here is something,' he said vehemently, 'which would make you open your sceptical eyes in astonishment.'

When he was excited his voice betrayed his northern ancestry, and that to Jim Bartholomew was a danger sign.

'My dear chap, it is a very excellent study indeed,' he said, 'and I congratulate you. Why, when I was in the Naval Intelligence Department, I had serious thoughts of taking up detective work myself.'

Again Mr Sanderson raised his eyes to the clock.

'You'll be going now,' he said pointedly, and Jim with a laugh turned out of the bank.

His horse, held by the ostler of the Royal Inn, was waiting by the sidewalk, and he mounted and cantered through the town and up the long slope which leads to the edge of the moor. Clearing the scatter of villas, he came at last after a stiff climb to the depression which was locally named the Devil's Bowl.

On the furthermost edge of the bowl a figure on horseback was waiting, silhouetted against the westering sun, and he shook up his mount and took a short cut down the rough slope and through the boulder-strewn bed of the hollow.

The girl who awaited him had been sitting astride, but now she had taken a more comfortable attitude, slipping one polished boot from the stirrup and throwing it across the horse's neck. She sat clasping her knee, and looking down at Jim's awkward progress with a smile of amusement.

Margot Cameron had the type of face which the black-and-white artists of France alone know how to draw. If she gave the impression of pallor, it was because of those vivid red lips of hers which drew all colour to her mouth and made the healthy pink and the faint tan of her face seem colourless by comparison.

When you were nearer to her you saw that the red of lip and the apparent pallor of skin owed no more to the reinforcement of art than the mop of gold-brown hair (now braided sedately) upon her shapely head.

Jim rode up, hat in hand, waving a salute.

'Do you know,' said the girl, dropping her right foot back into the stirrup, 'that whilst I was sitting here there came over me, with almost stunning force, the realisation that you *do* work for a living after all!'

'I keep office hours,' said Jim smugly, 'which is quite a different thing. If you have been in England all this long time and have not discovered that English businessmen do not begin work until ten o'clock in the morning, that they knock off for tea at three o'clock in the afternoon, and go home at four, then your trip has been wasted.'

A gleam shone in the girl's eyes. She did not readily smile, and if laughing had been a habit of hers, such hours of her life as were spent in Bartholomew's company would have been a series of hysterical giggles.

They rode quietly side by side for a time before Jim spoke.

'Talking of hideous realisations,' he said slowly, 'it has been my day's obsession that I shall only see you once more after today – you still intend sailing on Saturday?'

The girl nodded.

'And you'll be away for–' He left his question half finished.

'I don't know,' said Margot shortly, 'my future plans are rather uncertain. For the moment they are largely determined by what course of action Frank and Cecile decide. They were talking of buying a place in England and staying here for a few years. Frank doesn't like the idea of my launching forth on my own, otherwise–' She stopped suddenly.

'Otherwise?' suggested Jim.

'Otherwise,' said the girl, 'I might, of course, think of taking a place myself in England.'

'Oh yes,' said Jim softly.

She turned to him.

'You wouldn't like me to do that, would you?' she asked abruptly, and Jim was silent.

'No,' he admitted in that quiet way of his, 'I don't think I should care for your taking that step. I should like it just to happen that you were here. If you weren't so infernally well off– I – I think your future might be planned a little more definitely.'

She waited, but he offered no explanation and she had not the will to demand one. They had reached the wild slope of the upper moor. Far away on the horizon like a tiny blue cloud was hoary Hay Tor, and beneath them, through the thin plantation that fringed the river, they glimpsed the silver fret of the Dart.

'This is the only place in England where I can breathe,' said the girl, snuffling the air.

'You have our permission,' said Jim graciously.

He pulled in his horse and pointed with his riding crop across the moor.

'Do you see that white house – it is not really a house, I think it was designed either for an emperor's shooting box or a lunatic asylum.'

'I see,' said the girl, shading her eyes.

'That is Tor Towers. I suppose you have met Mrs Markham?'

'Markham?' said the girl, wrinkling her forehead. 'No, I don't think I have.'

'She is a compatriot of yours and another immensely wealthy lady.'

'American?' said the girl in surprise. 'It is curious we haven't met her and we've been here for a year.'

'I've only seen her once myself,' admitted Jim. 'She is a client of the bank, but Sanderson usually interviews her.'

'Is she young or old?'

'Quite young,' said Jim enthusiastically, 'and as beautiful as – as, well, have you ever seen Greuze's picture in the Louvre, 'L'Oiseau Mort'? Well, she's as beautiful as that, and Greuze might have painted his picture with her as a model except for the darkness of her hair.'

The girl was looking at him, her eyebrows arched with something that might have been amusement and was certainly surprise.

'Tut – tut!' she said with mock severity, 'this enthusiasm–'

'Don't be silly, Margot,' said Jim, and he really did blush. 'I only saw her once, I tell you.'

'Once? But she made an impression

apparently,' nodded the girl.

'In a way she did,' said Jim, returning to his old seriousness, 'and in a way she didn't.'

'I understand you perfectly,' said the girl. 'What do you mean?'

'I mean I could admire her and yet there was something about her which left me with an odd sense of sadness.'

Margot laughed shortly.

'Of all ways to a man's heart, an odd sense of sadness is the shortest,' she said. 'Come, let us get home.'

She turned her horse to one of the smaller roads leading to the valley of the Dart and the Moor ford from which the town took its name.

'Wait a bit.'

Jim reined his horse to a standstill, and Margot Cameron turning back saw something in his face that set her heart thumping more than the exercise of reining in her horse justified.

'Margot, I'm not going to see a great deal more of you,' said Jim and his voice was husky. 'You're going away and God knows when you're coming back again. And when you've left, this place which you and I think is so beautiful will be just a damnable desert – if you will pardon the profanity.'

She did not speak, but looked past him.

'I think I'm staying on in this town,' he said, 'because I am probably doing the only kind of job that I'm fit for. And it is likely that I shall stay here for ever and be a bald old bank manager at seventy. I wasn't intended to be a bank manager,' he said, with a return to his whimsical self, 'it was never ordained that I should sit in an office behind a leather-covered table and call the bluff on people who want a thousand overdraft on a five-hundred security. It was intended that I should be a sailor,' he said half to himself, 'or a – yes, a bank robber! I have a criminal heart, but I have no enterprise.'

'What is this all leading to?' asked the girl, bringing up her eyes to his face.

'It is leading to this one vital and important fact,' said Jim, sitting bolt upright on his horse, a sure sign of his nervousness. 'It means that I love you and I don't want you to leave this country in any ignorance of that point. Wait a moment,' he said, as he thought she was about to speak (as a matter of fact she found a little difficulty in breathing in spite of her testimonial to the qualities of Dartmoor), 'I know you'll tell me that you wish I hadn't told you, but after all you'll wish that because you will be afraid of my hurt.'

He shook his head.

'I've got the hurt and I'm getting rid of a lot of my mind-sickness when I tell you that I love you. I'm not going to ask you to be my wife either, Margot. It would be unfair to entertain the idea of marrying you, even supposing you did not whack me over the head with your crop at the bare suggestion. I just wanted to tell you that I love you and that I'm going to work – I shall leave this grisly town ... and some day perhaps...' His speech tailed off into something like incoherence.

She was laughing softly, though there was a suspicion of tears in her eyes.

'You are a queer man, Jim,' she said softly; 'and now having proposed to me and rejected yourself, nothing remains for me to say except that I will never be a sister to you and that I promised Cecile I would bring you home to tea.'

Jim swallowed something and then with a deep sigh stuck his heels into his horse and pushed him forward to the girl's side.

'That's that,' he said.

'I wonder if your that is my that?' said the girl, and went on quickly. 'Now, let us gossip about the beautiful Mrs Markham.'

And of the beautiful Mrs Markham and other matters they talked until they passed through the stone pillars of Moor House, that quaint mansion on the fringe of Moorford which the Camerons had rented for the summer.

2

Frank, a tall handsome American of thirty-five, was coming back from the tennis court, and he greeted Jim and his sister from afar.

'I've had a visit from your assistant,' he said, after the horses had been taken away and Margot had gone into the house.

'From Sanderson?' said Jim in astonishment, 'what the dickens did he want? Have you overdrawn your account?'

Frank grinned.

'Nothing so prosaic as that,' he said. 'No, it was on quite an interesting business he came. By the way, he's something of an amateur detective, I suppose you know?'

Jim groaned.

'Good Lord!' he said dismally, 'he hasn't been up here rustling clues or anything of that kind, has he?'

The other laughed.

'Not exactly,' he said, 'but a month ago he asked me for an introduction to a personal friend of mine. I happened to mention when I was talking with Sanderson at the bank that John Rogers, our District Attorney, was a friend of mine. Rogers has an extraordinary knowledge of criminals and has quite the best library on criminology in the United States. This was the fact I let fall to your Mr Sanderson and which resulted in my giving him a letter of introduction to John and his consequent visit today to see me. Apparently John has put him in possession of important data and Sanderson wished one or two matters explained – such as the functions of our State Governors and their power to grant pardons.'

'What is he after?' asked Jim after a puzzling moment. 'He never confides in me, you know; in fact, I rather jibe him about his criminal investigations, and, in consequence, we are not exactly the most intimate of friends.'

Frank had led the way to his den as they were talking. He took up a sheet of notepaper from his table and read it over.

'I jotted down a few items after he had gone,' he said, 'and really, Bartholomew, your Mr Sanderson isn't as eccentric as he seems. This is the point. There is in England at this present moment what he romantically calls "The Big Four of Crime." Three of them are citizens of my own dear native land, and one, I believe, is a Wop – or a Spaniard – who poses as an Italian, named Romano. The fact that Romano is a criminal has been established. The other three, about whom there are known records, are a Mr and Mrs Trenton – Doc. Trenton is the man – I've got most of these facts from Sanderson – and a particularly well-experienced forger named Talbot. These are the names by which they call themselves, of course, and I wouldn't vouch for their accuracy.'

'But what on earth has this to do–' began Jim.

'Wait a bit,' said Frank, 'I want to tell you this much. I think your man has got on the right track. There's no doubt whatever about the existence of the four persons whose doings he is following. They are very much alive and kicking. The police of most of the countries in Europe, certainly the police of America, know them and their exploits very well, for at one time or another they have all been in the hands of the law. The work that Sanderson has been engaged upon, apparently, has been the identification of these four law breakers with a gang which, for the past year, has been engaged in jewel robberies in Paris and London.'

Jim Bartholomew nodded.

'I have good reason for knowing there is such a gang,' he said. 'Almost every post from the Bankers' Association contains some fresh warning and some new particular of their methods. I suppose it was from these "confidentials" that Sanderson got his idea?'

The 'confidentials' were the secret documents which bankers in all countries receive, not only from their own associates but from the police headquarters.

'He told me as much,' said Frank. 'What Sanderson had really been doing is this. He has been canvassing the police forces of the world by correspondence, getting particulars of the jewel and bank thieves known to them and, when it is possible, their photographs. That is why I was able to help him with my friend the District Attorney, who has written to Sanderson telling him that he has sent him on a batch of information and photographs. They hadn't turned up when Sanderson came here, but the American mail comes in scraps, as you probably know.'

'What is Sanderson's idea as to the future?' asked Jim, puzzled. 'Does he aspire to be a policeman? I suppose he didn't take you that much into his confidence?'

Frank laughed.

'That is just what he did,' he said. 'As a matter of fact, he unbosomed himself of his ambitions in a most highly confidential way, but as he did not extract from me any promise that I would not pass the information on I can tell you. I can rely upon you, Bartholomew, not to rag him?'

'Of course,' protested Jim. 'Had I known he was taking the thing so seriously and doing such excellent work I would have given him all the assistance in my power.'

'Sanderson's idea, and his chief ambition, is to create a Bankers' Protection Corps,' Frank went on, 'and it is quite an excellent scheme. His plan is to take the likeliest men from the banking world, clerks and so on, and train them to the detection of banking crimes – and here comes Jones to call us to tea.'

He rose, and Jim preceded him from the room. In the hall Frank Cameron changed the subject abruptly.

'I shall miss you quite a lot,' he said, 'and I am hoping that fate will bring us back to this delightful spot.'

Jim was as fervently hoping the same, but did no more than murmur a conventional agreement.

'The voyage is going to do my wife a lot of

good, I hope. She has not been quite the same since her sister died.'

It was the first time that Frank Cameron had mentioned his wife's illness, though Jim had had many talks with Margot on the matter.

'She died quite suddenly in the United States, didn't she?'

Frank nodded.

'Yes, we were in Paris at the time. One morning we got an urgent cable and Cecile went back to New York next day – she insisted upon going alone – she arrived there just in time, poor girl. She has never quite recovered from the shock. It has clouded her life most tragically – by the way, you never talk to Cecile about her sister, do you?'

Jim shook his head.

'No, I have never mentioned her, and it is not a subject I should care to raise.'

Frank nodded his approval.

Margot had changed from her riding kit and was sitting in the drawing-room with her sister-in-law. Mrs Cameron rose and came towards him with outstretched hands. She was a stately, pretty woman of thirty with flawless features and dark eyes that had always seemed to Frank to hold the shadow of tragedy.

'Thank heaven, I've finished my packing,' she said.

'When and how do you leave?' asked Jim. 'Tomorrow?'

'Early on Saturday morning,' said Cecile Cameron, handing him his tea. 'We're going by car to Southampton and sending the baggage on overnight. I want to stay here until the very last moment and it will be rather fun motoring in the early morning.'

'I have ordered fabulous sums to be at your disposal tomorrow,' laughed Jim. 'I don't know what my general manager will say when he knows that the bank has lost four such excellent clients.'

'Four?' said Mrs Cameron. 'Who else is leaving beside us three?'

'Mrs Markham of Tor Towers will be a fellow passenger of yours – and she's American, by the way.'

'Markham? Do you know her, Frank?'

Frank Cameron shook his head.

'She is not a New Yorker,' explained Jim. 'I believe she comes from Virginia. She is a regular visitor to this country, and as a matter of fact she is coming back to us and has deposited her jewels with us – I wish she hadn't. I hate the responsibility of carrying a hundred thousand pounds' worth of diamonds in my vault, and as soon as the good lady is on the sea I shall send them up to London for safe custody.'

'Mrs Markham,' said Frank thoughtfully. 'It is curious we have never met her. Is she young or old?'

'Young,' said Jim. 'I have never seen her myself, except at a distance. She leaves the management of her domestic affairs to her butler, a pompous gentleman named Winter – a typical superior domestic servant. Sanderson has conducted all the business dealings we have had with Mrs Markham, so I know very little about her, except that she is a most agreeable lady, has tons of money, is a widow, and spends most of her time painting sketches of Dartmoor. But I don't suppose you three good people will want any fourth, and certainly you'll find scores of friends on the ship. Have you a suite?'

Frank nodded.

'We have Suite B, which is the best on the ship, and Cecile has a great friend going out, Mrs Dupreid – Jane is sailing, isn't she?' He turned to his wife.

'Yes, I had a letter from her this morning. You're quite right, Mr Bartholomew, one doesn't want a great crowd on a ship, and sea voyages depress me horribly. I don't think Jane Dupreid is going to be much of an acquisition to our party, Frank.' She smiled quietly. 'Jane is a bad sailor and takes to her bunk the moment the ship leaves the wharf and stays there until it passes Sandy Hook.'

The conversation drifted to ships and passengers and their eccentricities, and was mainly between Frank Cameron and his wife and Jim. Margot Cameron was unusually silent and thoughtful, and it was Cecile who drew attention to the fact.

'You're rather quiet, Margot; what is the matter?'

Margot Cameron roused from her reverie with a start.

'How terrible that my silences are remarkable!' she said, with a little laugh. 'I suppose it is rather like when the engine stops at sea, it wakes you up! To be perfectly frank, I was feeling a little sad at leaving this place.'

Frank looked from his sister to Jim and back to his sister again and smiled.

'Oh yes,' he said dryly.

'I think I must be getting old,' said Margot, 'but somehow of late I hate change.'

'I rather dislike it myself,' said Frank, 'but either you or I have got to go, Margot. We have to settle up Aunt Martha's estate.'

He saw Jim's eyes light up and grinned.

'That sounds as though we are going to make a short stay and then home again, but I really ought to see the mining properties I am interested in and that means spending the winter in California.'

Jim groaned.

'Well,' he said grimly, 'you'll find me here with the other permanent fixtures of the town, and maybe when you return you will find plates affixed to various buildings to commemorate your stay. I shall be a deadly dull man.'

'Perhaps a circus will happen along,' suggested Margot helpfully.

'There are two courses open to me,' said the solemn Jim. 'The first is to allow myself to get into the whirl of local gaiety and take up sheep breeding, and the second is to rob the bank and shoot up the town. There is every incentive to rob the bank,' he added thoughtfully. 'The beautiful Mrs Markham's diamonds–'

'Why do you always prefix Mrs Markham with the word "beautiful"?' asked the girl, not without a certain undercurrent of irritation.

'For lack of a better adjective,' was the cryptic reply.

'Well, I shouldn't shoot up the town until we're well on our way,' said Frank, passing his cup back to Cecile.

'Phew!' said Jim suddenly, 'what a wonderful ring!'

He was looking at Mrs Cameron's outstretched hand and she flushed slightly.

'It is lovely, isn't it?' said Cameron quietly. 'Let me show it to Bartholomew.'

She hesitated, then drew the ring from her finger and handed it to the visitor.

It was a broad band of gold and had the appearance of having been cut rather than moulded. It was the design which had attracted Bartholomew's attention, and now he carried it to the window to examine it more carefully. For the design was an unusual one. Three serpent-headed women, delicately and beautifully carved, every line of their sombre faces exquisitely modelled, though each face was not more than an eighth of an inch in length.

He examined it admiringly, noted the twining snakes and a hint of wings, and brought the ring back to Mrs Cameron.

'The Daughters of the Night,' he said. 'A beautiful piece of work!'

'The Daughters of the Night?' Mrs Cameron frowned.

'Yes, they are the three Furies, aren't they? The Roman deities who brought punishment to evil-doers.'

'I never heard them called the Daughters of the Night.' Cecile Cameron spoke slowly as she replaced the ring on her finger. 'The Daughters of the Night!'

'My mythology is a little bit rusty,' smiled Jim, 'but that is the name by which I remember them. It is certainly a lovely piece of work.'

'You are fortunate to see it,' said Frank. 'My wife only wears it one day in the year, the anniversary of her father's death. Isn't that so, darling?'

Mrs Cameron nodded.

'Father gave one to my sister and myself,' she said. 'He was a great connoisseur and had had this ring copied from one which is now in the Louvre. It hasn't' – she faltered – 'it hasn't very pleasant memories, but Daddy was so proud of them – it was his own work – that I wear mine once a year for his sake.'

She did not mention her dead sister, but Jim guessed that that was where the unhappiness of the memory lay.

'It is rather valuable,' said Jim, 'because the ring at the Louvre was stolen in '99 if you remember, and today this is the only copy in the world.'

Margot had risen and walked to the piano and was playing softly, and Jim had come to accept Margot's playing as part of the daily pleasure which life held for him. He pulled up a chair to her side.

'Play me something that will soothe my jagged nerves,' he said.

'You've no right to have jagged nerves – a boy like you,' she said, and stopped.

'This time next week where shall we be?' quoth he. 'What ship are you going on?'

'On the *Ceramia*.'

'On the *Ceramia?*' he lifted his eyebrows. 'Great Scott! Old man Stornoway is chief officer and old Smythe is chief engineer.'

She turned on the stool, her hands on her lap.

'And who may these old gentlemen be?' she asked. 'Frank!' she called over her shoulder, 'Come and hear about the doddering friends of Mr Bartholomew.'

'Well, they're not really old men,' explained Jim, 'but they are very great pals of mine. You see, during the war I was in the Navy. I was almost everything that you can be in the Navy, from stoker to Intelligence Officer. Stornoway was the skipper of B. 75, which was a special service destroyer, and I was Intelligence Officer on her. We were running a patrol to the north of Scotland. Smythe was chief engineer and so we got to know one another rather well, and when we were picked up–'

'Picked up?' said the girl. 'What do you mean?'

'Well, you see, we were torpedoed rather neatly one cold February day, and we three were in the water together for about twelve hours, and naturally under those circumstances you get to know a man.'

The girl laughed.

'Did you rescue them from a watery grave?' she asked sardonically. 'Or did they rescue you?'

'Well, we sort of rescued one another,' explained Jim hazily.

The girl sensed behind that awkward statement a story of unrecorded heroism and resolved to seek out Stornoway at the earliest opportunity and discover the truth of this incident.

Jim would have stayed to dinner but for the fact that he had a long report which must be written that night, and the girl walked with him down the drive.

'So you're going to be a bank robber after

I leave, are you?' she said.

'Why not?' he protested stoutly. 'It's easy. Do you know, Margot, I have a criminal mind.'

'I've often suspected you of having a weak mind, but never a criminal mind,' said the girl, 'but I suppose that–'

'In what respect have I a weak mind?'

'Well,' she drawled, 'I think you lack resolution, and in some respects self-confidence.'

'Good lord!' he gasped. 'I thought I was the most sure and certain man in the world.'

'In some respects you are. In fact, in some respects you are inclined to be bumptious,' she went on remorselessly, 'but in others–'

He stopped and faced her.

'Now you've got to tell me where I've failed. Don't leave me in this benighted land – for benighted it will be when you have gone – with that untold mystery taxing all my mental resources. In what respect have I failed?'

'I think you're very – English,' she said.

'In other words, pudden-headed,' said Jim. 'But surely you are not going to blame me because I am a citizen of the most downtrodden race in the world.'

She laughed.

'I think you're dense, that's all.'

'Oh, is that all?' he said sarcastically. And then more seriously. 'Suppose I am willingly dense. Suppose I know that within my reach is the greatest prize in all the world?' His voice shook ever so slightly. 'Suppose I know there is somebody so generous and so fine and so immensely gracious that she would give herself to me – I who have just enough money to realise my poverty. Suppose I knew all this and had resolved in my heart that for her happiness and mine I must come to her with an accomplishment behind me, would you say that I lacked confidence?'

She did not speak, but laid her hand within his, and in silence they walked the rest of the way.

'I shall see you tomorrow,' she said without looking at him. 'You wouldn't like to come to Southampton to see us off?'

'That's an idea,' he said. 'It will be rather painful, but I – yes, I'll do it. I'll come down by the morning train.'

'Why not come down by car with us?'

'I can't do that,' he said. 'I am due in London on Saturday morning, but I'll go up by the midnight train to London, see my general manager, and catch the boat train to

Southampton. Good night!' He held out his hand and she looked round.

Behind them the groom was leading Jim's horse.

'Good night,' she said, 'and don't bring your horse tomorrow. I can't go riding.'

'Will you come into town tomorrow with your sister?' he asked.

'Possibly,' she nodded.

He swung into his saddle and the girl was gently rubbing the nose of the horse.

'Jim,' she asked suddenly, 'if – if you are going to make your fortune ... you will try something very rapid, won't you?'

He stooped over and laid his hand upon her head and she raised her eyes to his.

'It will be something infernally rapid,' he said.

3

Mr Stephen Sanderson had had a bulky letter by the American mail and had sat up half the night writing, taking notes and comparing the new data he had received from Frank Cameron's friend with the voluminous matter he had already classified and tabulated.

It was a long work, but it was a labour of love for Stephen Sanderson. It meant the careful reading of thousands of newspaper extracts dealing with the wave of crime which had swept over England and France that year. It meant the comparison of methods thus recorded, with those which had been supplied him by the report which had come from New York. He had worked until the daylight filtered greyly through the curtained window, with a dozen portraits of men and women outspread on the table before him. He was piecing together with amazing patience the pieces of the most fascinating jigsaw puzzle.

Only one or two pieces did not fit, and he

arose after four hours' sleep, refreshed and thrilled by the thought that even these elusive scraps might yet be fitted into the picture.

Jim, coming to the office at ten o'clock, found his assistant sitting before his desk a little hollow-eyed but more cheerful than he remembered him.

'Good morning, Mr Sanderson.'

'Good morning, Mr Bartholomew.'

Jim had an inquiry on the tip of his tongue, but checked himself. He looked at his assistant with a new respect.

'Is there anything particularly interesting this morning?' asked Jim as he hung up his hat and slipped off his coat – it had been raining that morning.

'Nothing, sir,' said Sanderson.

He was punctilious in all outward evidence of respect.

'I have the money ready for Mrs Cameron and for Mrs Markham.'

'Oh yes, but she's not drawing out her balance, is she?'

'Yes, sir,' said the other. 'Her balance isn't a very large one. About £2,000. She is leaving a little in the account because she is returning. I am expecting Mr Winter any moment. Would you like to see him?'

'Who is Winter? Oh, the butler? No, thank you very much,' said Jim carelessly. 'If he wants to see me he'll find me in the office.'

He went into his room, closed the door, and Sanderson went on with his work. There was a knock at the door and the clerk came in.

'Mr Winter, sir,' he said.

'Oh, I'll see him in here. Ask him in, will you?'

A stout, genial-looking man with black side whiskers was Mr Winter. He offered his large hand, and sitting down on the seat opposite Sanderson at the manager's invitation, he produced a pink slip which Sanderson examined.

'Well, Mr Winter, I suppose your lady is in a state of great excitement about the prospect of going back to America?'

'No, sir,' smiled Mr Winter. 'There's very little excitement at Tor Towers, sir, believe me. It is just about the dullest situation I was ever in. Mind you, everything is as it should be in the way of food and accommodation, but there's precious little life.'

'When are you leaving?'

'Tonight, sir. We are going by car to Bournemouth and on early tomorrow to the ship.'

'It is going to be a pleasant trip for you, Mr Winter.'

The elder man rubbed the bald patch on the top of his head.

'Well, sir, it may be and it may not,' he said cautiously. 'I have never been out of England and I don't know how I'm going to get on with these Americans. Of course, Mrs M. is a very nice lady, and if they are all like her I shall be comfortable. But never having been abroad or been on a ship – why, naturally I'm a bit nervous.'

'You'll be all right,' said Sanderson.

He rang the bell and handed the cheque to the clerk.

'Bring the cash for this, will you,' he said.

'There is one thing, sir,' the butler leant over the table and lowered his voice. 'Mrs M. is a little nervous about those jewels you've got and she asked me if I'd have a look at them to see if they are properly packed – in fact, sir, I won't tell a lie, to see if they are still in your possession.'

Sanderson indulged in one of his rare smiles.

'I don't think she need worry about that,' he said. 'I suppose it is the jewel robberies which are worrying her?'

'That's it, sir,' nodded Winter emphatically. 'My lady says that she was robbed once before when she was in America and it has made her scared.'

'I think I can put her mind at rest,' said Sanderson, rising, and going to a steel door at the end of his room.

He manipulated two keys and presently the big door swung open, and he disappeared into the vault.

He came back in a moment with a small brown-paper parcel.

'Do you want me to open this?' he said, pointing to the package and the sealed tape which enveloped it.

'No, sir,' said Winter. 'All she wanted you to do was to tear the paper so that I could see. I understand the jewels are in a glass case.'

'Mrs Markham's idea,' said Sanderson, 'and not a bad one.'

He caught a corner of the paper and tore it cautiously, revealing an oblong glass box.

'There they are.'

Mr Winter leaned forward and looked reverently at a section of a broad diamond collar which sparkled and glittered in the light.

'That's all right, sir,' he said, 'and here's Mrs Markham's seal.'

He handed over a gummed label, across which was written 'Stella Markham' and the date.

'What is that for?' asked Sanderson in surprise, and Mr Winter chuckled.

'A wonderful lady is Mrs M. She thinks of everything. "Winter," she said, "after Mr Sanderson has torn the paper you'd better put this label over the tear so that nobody will think the parcel has been interfered with without my knowledge."'

He licked the label and with an 'excuse me, sir' rubbed it down over the torn paper.

'There's a gentleman Mrs Markham doesn't like,' he said, with a jerk of his head to the window which gave out upon the High Street.

Following the direction of his eyes Sanderson saw the back of a stocky figure.

'Who is that?' he asked.

'That's Farmer Gold. He's a very objectionable man and turned madame off his property where she was sketching.'

'He's usually a very decent fellow,' said Sanderson. 'I'll put this package back in the vaults and you can reassure Mrs Markham that her jewels are safe.'

The clerk came in with the money, which was counted, not once, but three times by the careful Mr Winter. He had pocketed the money and was rising when Sanderson detained him.

'There's one thing I want to see you about, Mr Winter,' he said, 'if you can spare five minutes of your time.'

'With all the pleasure in life,' said Mr Winter.

'You're going to America, and you will be in a favourable position to collect a little information for me, especially whilst you are on the ship.'

'If I'm well enough to get about, sir,' interrupted Winter. 'I'm not looking forward–'

'Oh, you'll be well enough to get about,' said Mr Sanderson, with a little laugh. 'Sailing with you will be Mr and Mrs Cameron.'

'Cameron?' repeated the other.

'Yes.'

'Are they country people? Do I know them?'

'I don't know whether you know them, but they live in this town.'

'Oh yes, the American people,' nodded Winter. 'Yes, sir.'

And Sanderson detailed his commission. Not for five minutes, but for twenty did he speak. It was necessary to some extent to take the butler into his confidence, and this

44

he did. Jim heard the murmur of voices in the next room and, looking across the un-frosted top of the door panel, caught a glimpse of Sanderson's earnest face and smiled.

He sealed the letter he was writing and passed into the outer office.

'Has Mrs Cameron been?' he asked his clerk.

'No, sir. Mr Winter, Mrs Markham's butler, is here.'

'Tell Mr Sanderson I shall be back in ten minutes,' said Jim, and went out into the High Street.

He was restless, impatient of things, crav-ing unreasonably for a glimpse of the face which was soon to pass away from him, perhaps for ever. He walked through the town in the direction of the Camerons' house and knew himself for a fool. He was halfway up Moor Hill when he saw the car coming slowly down. It stopped at his signal and Cecile Cameron beckoned him.

'Where are you going so early?' he asked.

The other occupant of the car was Mar-got, who had no need to make any inquiry and was only interested in what excuse Jim would invent.

'I was coming out to meet you,' said Jim,

seating himself in one of the bucket seats.

'And Margot?' said Cecile softly.

'And Margot,' Jim admitted without blushing. 'I know I am a frantic idiot, but I just hate your going.'

'I think we all wish we were staying,' said Cecile, 'even Margot.'

'Even Margot,' scoffed her sister-in-law.

'Can't you find an excuse to come with us?' said Mrs Cameron.

'I found the excuse quite a long time ago,' said Jim.

Margot stared out of the window, interested apparently in anything and everything except the young man in tweeds who sat with his foot against hers.

'Maybe I'll turn up there if you don't come back quickly,' Jim went on. 'One of these fine days when you're sitting in your palatial apartment on the 29th floor of the Goldrox Hotel you will ring your bell for the waiter and in will come Jim Bartholomew – I had no idea I had walked such a short distance.'

The car was pulling up before the bank.

Sanderson was standing at the door talking to his visitor.

'And now to do a little honest banking business,' said Jim. 'I–'

He stopped dead at the sight of Mrs Cameron's face. It was as white as death, her lips were bloodless and her face was frozen in an expression of horror.

Jim turned and saw Sanderson at the door. He had just given his final word to Mrs Markham's butler and had not noticed the arrival of the car. He looked back again at Cecile. She was shaking as if from an ague.

'My God!' she gasped. 'Oh, my God!'

By this time Sanderson had turned into the bank.

'What is the matter, Cecile dear? For heaven's sake, what has happened?' said Margot, putting her arms about Cecile.

'Nothing, nothing.'

Jim was dumb with astonishment.

Sanderson! What was there in the sight of that stony face which would reduce this well-poised woman to such a condition of terror? That it was Sanderson he did not doubt. He jumped out of the car and assisted Mrs Cameron into the bank.

'Oh, it is nothing; I am stupid,' she said faintly, as he brought her into his office. 'Just a little fainting attack, I sometimes have them. You must please forgive me, Mr Bartholomew, for making such a spectacle

47

of myself.'

'But what was it, dear?' Margot asked anxiously.

'Nothing, nothing.' Mrs Cameron forced a smile. 'Really it was nothing, Margot. I just had an attack of the vapours. Will you attend to me, Mr Bartholomew? I – I don't think I want to see your assistant manager.'

Jim was only too anxious to deal with the matter himself. He walked into Sanderson's office and that worthy was at the table apparently unconscious of his responsibility for Mrs Cameron's condition.

'I am attending to Mrs Cameron's account myself, Sanderson,' said Jim.

'Very good, sir,' replied the other, without looking up. 'I've just fixed Mrs Markham's account.'

In three minutes Jim was back in his office with the notes and by that time Cecile Cameron had recovered something of her calm.

'There's quite a run on the bank today,' said Jim.

'Mrs Markham's butler has just drawn £2,000 for that lady.'

There was a silence as he counted the money, then: 'Mrs Markham is the lady who is going to America, is she?' said Cecile.

'I believe she is leaving today or tomorrow. I'll find out.'

He went into Sanderson's room. He guessed that Cecile's interest in Mrs Markham was an excuse to get him out of the room that she might have a little further time to recover and he delayed his return as long as possible.

He was somewhat surprised to find his assistant in excellent humour and informative.

'Yes,' said Jim on his return, 'she's sailing tomorrow and her butler has been confiding his terrors of the sea to Sanderson. I gather she is leaving today.'

He saw the girls back to their car and bade farewell to them and stood watching the number plate at the back of the car until it had disappeared, then he went slowly back to his office. He pressed the bell which communicated with Sanderson and the assistant manager came in.

'Sanderson,' he said, 'I owe you an apology.'

'Do you, sir?' said Sanderson in surprise.

'Yes,' said Jim. 'I've been rather a boor about your little hobby and I didn't realise how very important your work in that direction may be?'

Mr Sanderson looked at him suspiciously.

'Of course, Mr Bartholomew, if you're going to be funny about it–'

'I'm not being funny at all,' said Jim. 'Sit down. I had a long talk with Mr Cameron yesterday afternoon, and without betraying any of your secrets he told me that you were working systematically with the object of identifying the members of the Big Four who have been victimising the banks.'

'Well, sir, that's true,' said Sanderson, sitting down, 'and I'm happy to say that I'm on the track. And I'm not the only one looking for them either,' he said. 'I had a letter yesterday from a friend of Mr Cameron's who's a lawyer in America, and he gave me some very interesting information. The biggest enemy to the Big Four is a woman – a woman detective who has been employed by the Department of Justice in America for four years tracking down the principal members. I don't know the name of the lady, and this fact was told me in confidence.'

'A woman detective sounds thrilling,' said Jim. 'What do you think are the prospects of their capture?'

Sanderson shook his head.

'That's a difficult question to answer,' he

said. 'As likely as not the lady who is on their track is nearer to detecting them than ever I shall be. She has unlimited resources, she has the Government of America behind her, she can appear in all sorts of guises, and can devote the whole of her time to the work.'

It seemed at that moment to Jim that he had a deeper grudge against the mysterious woman detective with her unlimited authority than he had against the miscreants whose undoing he sought.

'By the way, sir, Mr Winter wanted to see Mrs Markham's jewels before he left,' said Sanderson as he was leaving, and gave an account of the interview.

He made no reference, however, to the interview which followed when they sat head to head over the table, he and the butler whom he was training and from whom he anticipated receiving such assistance.

'Blow her jewellery,' said Jim. 'I wish to heaven she'd leave it in London or some-where. I'll have to send that necklace to town just as soon as Mrs Markham has gone, Sanderson. You might write to the Head Office and tell them that they can expect it on Tuesday and you can take it. A trip to town will do you no harm, and it will probably help you.'

Sanderson nodded gratefully.

'Thank you, sir, I want to go to Scotland Yard to see Inspector McGinty. I have had some correspondence with him. He seems a very intelligent man.'

'He probably is,' said Jim dryly. 'It is curious how often real detectives are that way!'

4

He had the choice of going home and eating a solitary lunch or mooning in his office. Somehow a meal, and a solitary meal, had no attraction for him and he was still in a state of indecision when he saw the Camerons' car pull up and Frank jump down.

Jim Bartholomew hurried out to meet him.

'I want to speak to you, Jim,' said that troubled man.

It was the first time he had called Jim Bartholomew by his Christian name, and Jim accepted the omen with pleasure.

'I can't make out what has happened to Cecile,' said Frank as they paced the broad sidewalk, deserted at the luncheon hour. 'This morning she was quite cheerful and even made a jest about that ring of hers, which is a mighty solemn subject with Cecile, I can tell you. What did you call it?'

'The Daughters of the Night,' said Jim. 'It sounds romantic and a little improper, but it is historically accurate.'

'Well, as I say, she went away from the house cheerful,' Frank went on, 'but came back from the bank a pitiful wreck. What happened?'

'The Lord knows!' said Jim. 'I was sitting in the car with her when suddenly I saw her face go white and I thought she was going to faint.'

'Was there any reason for it?'

'None that I could see,' said Jim, who thought it wisest not to mention the fact that it was apparently the sight of Sanderson which had reduced her to this condition.

'Well, anyway, she's decided that she won't go to America tomorrow.'

'Good Lord!' said Jim, and his heart leapt.

'I can't go either, of course,' said Frank. 'But Margot will have to go. There are documents to be signed and either she or I must sign them. We'll follow on after.'

'Is Margot going alone?' said Jim.

'I'm afraid she must,' replied the other. 'She'll have plenty of room to move around. I've engaged a suite for three.'

'What does she say about it?'

'Of course, she's very much distressed,' said Frank, 'and I'd like you to see her. She's a good girl that, Bartholomew, the best in the world is my little sister. She's leaving tonight for Southampton. I wish you would go down and see her off tomorrow. I do not like to leave Cecile in her present condition.'

'Rather,' said Jim, with alacrity. 'You haven't any idea what has decided Mrs Cameron not to go? I thought she was rather keen on the trip.'

'She was never enthusiastic,' said the other, 'but she was agreeable. You see, her friend was going out, Mrs Dupreid, and there were all the prospects of rather a jolly voyage. I'm as sick as a monkey about it. What made her decide to change her mind heaven only knows. I never attempt to pry into first causes, so far as women are concerned, and in consequence I am a happily married man.'

Jim laughed.

'Can you spare time to come up to the house now?' asked Cameron. 'My car is here.'

Jim hesitated.

'Just one moment.'

He went back into the bank and entered Sanderson's room.

'I'm going out for about an hour, Sanderson,' he said; 'if you want me will you 'phone Mrs Cameron's house.'

Sanderson nodded. He was even genial.

'I don't suppose you'll be needed this afternoon, Mr Bartholomew. I've settled the trouble about Jackson & Wales' bill, and the statement will be ready for you to sign at five.'

On the way up to Moor House Frank Cameron offered Jim more of his confidence than he had shown during the twelve months of their friendship.

'Cecile has never been herself since her sister's death. She died of typhoid in New York City,' he said. 'I told you Cecile got there in time and only just in time. They were rather a devoted family and I sometimes wonder whether the shock has not affected her mind – I'll be candid with you, Jim. It worries me to death at times. I insisted upon her seeing a specialist when we were in New York last fall and I gave him my views, but he could trace nothing of a serious nature and put her condition down to shock and nerve trouble. Margot, of course, has been a brick, as she always is in times of stress. How do you feel towards Margot?' he asked suddenly.

Jim went red.

'I love her,' he said suddenly and with strange gruffness.

'I thought so,' said the other quietly. 'Well,

56

what are you going to do about it?'

There was a half-smile on his face as he asked the question.

'I'm going to ask her to be my wife, but I'm going to ask her, not as a bank manager with a microscopic income–'

'You know that Margot has money of her own?' interrupted Frank.

'That is why,' said Jim quietly. 'I have infinite faith in my – my star, if you like. I am going to make good, and just as soon as Margot is on the way I shall resign my position as bank manager and take up something which offers better opportunities. I know, my dear chap, what you're going to say' – he laid his hand on the other's knee. 'You're going to tell me that you've the very job for me – I know you're a very rich man and I dare say you could place me in the way of getting easy money, but that isn't quite good enough and you wouldn't like me much if I accepted your offer.'

'You're right,' said Frank after a pause. 'And I respect you for it, Jim. I don't doubt that you'll pull through and I know somebody else who will share my faith.'

Lunch was waiting when they arrived, and Cecile Cameron, who had recovered something of her self-possession, met Jim with a whimsical smile.

'Well, what do you think of my latest eccentricity, Mr Bartholomew?'

'The knowledge that you are still keeping money in my bank compensates me for a lot,' said Jim. 'After all, is it eccentric to do what you want to do and not do the things you don't want to do? Is it not more eccentric to stop yourself doing what your heart aches to do?' He looked straight at Margot and Margot returned his gaze without flushing. 'To give up what you want most in the world.'

'I don't call that eccentric,' said the girl. 'I call that – a little heroic.'

Jim bowed, which was disconcerting.

'I decided that I couldn't break with this very peaceful life yet awhile,' said Mrs Cameron, 'and I really think that I ought not to be blamed.'

'Nobody is blaming you, darling,' said Frank. 'Would you like to go to the Continent for a little while?'

'I'd like to stay here,' said his wife quickly, 'in this little out-of-the-world place where one sees nobody.'

'This is where you bow again, Jim,' said Margot.

'Do you "Jim" Jim too?' asked Frank in

spurious amazement.

'Occasionally, in my tender moments,' said the girl coolly, and Jim choked.

It was an unexpectedly cheerful luncheon party, and Jim went to the bank with two conspicuous possibilities for future happiness. (1) That if the Camerons stayed, Margot would return. (2) That if Margot returned, he would never have the courage to let her go again. It is extraordinary how the prospect of his future cowardice cheered him.

Margot came to the bank that afternoon to say goodbye. She had probably chosen this public spot because she was not quite certain how she would behave if they parted in more secluded circumstances.

'Cecile is going away to Scotland. She had a long, long talk with Frank this afternoon,' said Margot. 'Frank came out of the study looking awfully serious. Anyway Cecile's gone. I've just seen her off.'

'Gone already?' said Jim in amazement. 'Has Frank–'

The girl shook her head.

'No, she's gone alone... She has some friends up there.'

'Poor girl, I wonder what it was.'

Margot looked at Jim.

'I've been trying to guess too. Did you notice that when she collapsed she was looking at your Mr Sanderson?'

Jim nodded.

'I did not fail to notice that,' he said. 'To my knowledge she had never seen Sanderson before.'

'I know she hadn't,' said the girl. 'We were talking about you two or three days ago and I was telling her about Mr Sanderson's detective hobby and she was amused. She then told me that she had never seen your manager.'

She offered Jim her hand.

'Goodbye, Jim,' she said gently. 'I think I shall be coming back soon.'

He took her hand in both of his and he found it difficult to speak.

'You understand, don't you?' he asked.

She nodded.

'I understand perfectly,' she replied. 'Won't you kiss me?'

She lifted up her face and he pressed her lips lightly with his.

5

Jim Bartholomew came back from the railway station with a heavy heart. He had declined Frank's offer to drive him to the bank and had promised to go up to the house to dinner. It accentuated his gloom that Sanderson was in an exuberantly cheerful mood. To Jim's intense annoyance he hummed little snatches of song as he worked, and the sound penetrating through wood and glass partition had the character of a dirge.

'What the devil are you moaning about?' demanded Jim, exploding into his assistant's room.

'Moaning, sir?' asked Sanderson, with a bland smile. 'I'm just happy, that's all. Do you know, sir, what the Big Four—'

'Oh, damn the Big Four!' growled Jim, irritably, and was surprised to hear the other chuckle.

He turned back from the door.

'Well, what about the Big Four?' he said, feeling that any subject which interested him that afternoon would be more than welcome.

'I've been piecing together the rewards offered for the capture of these fellows,' said Sanderson. 'Have you any idea how much it aggregates?'

'Not the faintest.'

'£120,000,' said Mr Sanderson impressively. 'The Italian Government alone offer £50,000 for the recovery of the Negretti diamonds. They are state heirlooms. The Duke of–'

'Shut up about money,' said Jim. 'Aren't you sick of talking pounds and dollars and francs and marks?'

'No, sir, I'm not,' said the other truthfully.

Jim had walked back in his room and Sanderson followed him.

'There's one thing I'd like to ask you to do, Mr Bartholomew,' he said.

'What's that?' asked Jim.

'Write to headquarters and ask them to let us have an extra revolver down here. We've only got one, the one in your desk. Do you know that I sleep on these premises, upstairs, absolutely unarmed?'

'Well, take mine,' said Jim. 'What a ferocious beggar you are! I think you go too often to the movies.'

'Movies? Me?' spluttered Sanderson indignantly. 'Do you imagine I spend my hard-earned money in that kind of trash? The only thing I have seen on the cinematograph, Mr Bartholomew,' he said emphatically, 'is a series of interesting photographs showing the life of the bee, and if these wretched cinema theatres would only show interesting topics of that character I should be a regular patron.'

'Here's the gun,' said Jim, unlocking the drawer and taking out a long-barrelled Colt. 'Be careful. It is loaded.'

'Put it in your drawer, sir, and leave the drawer unlocked and I'll take it tonight.'

'Why do you want a revolver?' asked Jim curiously.

'Because I have a feeling that sooner or later we are coming to grips with the Big Four,' replied Sanderson solemnly.

'Bosh!' said the sceptical Jim. 'What the dickens are the Big Four coming to this little burg for? To steal Jingle and Merrick's overdraft, or–'

'There's a hundred thousand pounds' worth of diamonds in this bank,' said Sanderson, significantly, and Jim whistled.

'By gosh! So there is! I think you're right. Now don't forget, Sanderson, those diamonds must go up to London on Tuesday.'

A customer came into the bank at that moment, a well-to-do farmer named Sturgeon who farmed about a thousand acres in the neighbourhood. He glanced up at the clock as he came in.

'I've just made it,' he said, putting down his paying-in book on the counter.

Jim, standing in the doorway of his room, gave him a nod.

'We're open day and night to take money, but we're rather careful of our business hours when it comes to paying out,' said Jim, his hands in his pockets.

'Hello, Bartholomew,' said Sturgeon. 'I saw a friend of yours half an hour ago getting out of the train at the Halt.'

The Halt, as its name implied, was a small station outside the town where the trains sometimes stopped to pick up and set down passengers who came from the moorland villages and could thus save a journey into town.

'I have so many friends that I can't place this particular one,' said Jim lazily

'Mrs Cameron,' was the surprising reply.

'Mrs Cameron? Nonsense,' said Jim incredulously. 'Mrs Cameron has gone up to London.'

'She may or may not have gone to town,' said the other. 'But I tell you that she got down at the Halt and got into her car which was waiting.'

Jim was silent.

'Maybe you're right,' he said at last.

'I am right,' smiled the other, gathering up his pass-book. 'So long!'

Jim Bartholomew went back into his room and closed the door.

Mrs Cameron had left by the three o'clock train which connected with the northern express at Bristol. She had gone an hour before Margot, who was catching the Exeter train connecting through Yeovil with Southampton.

He had held his breath for a moment, having a wild idea that it might have been Margot. But Mrs Cameron!

Frank would be able to explain, and he was on his way to the telephone when he thought better of it. Mrs Cameron would hardly change her plan again without making her husband aware of the fact. Then he remembered that Frank had spoken most casually of his wife going to Scotland and had offered no comment upon her decision. It was curious.

When he went up to dinner that night he

half expected to find Cecile Cameron sitting in the drawing-room, but she was not there and Frank made no mention of her, which was also an extraordinary circumstance, for Frank Cameron never tired of talking of his wife. It was a very dull meal and Jim missed Margot horribly. He talked of her very frankly and his host encouraged him. It seemed to Jim as though Frank Cameron was anxious to keep the conversation away from his wife, and once when Jim mentioned casually the difficulties Cecile might have in catching the Scottish express, Frank changed the subject.

Jim walked home that night, a little sick at heart, a little lonely and very love-conscious. A thin drizzle of rain was falling and he had left his raincoat at the office. His way back to the house where he lodged lay past the bank and he felt in his pocket for his key. It was there, he noted with satisfaction. He quickened his steps, overtaking another pedestrian, who turned out to be the inspector of the local police.

'A wretched night, Mr Bartholomew,' said that gentleman, recognising the other. 'Was that Mr Cameron's car I saw in the High Street half an hour ago? There it is now.'

He pointed to a red tail light on the

opposite side of the road.

'No, it is not Mr Cameron's car. Has it been there long?'

'About half an hour,' said the inspector. 'I suppose it is one of the gentry from the country. They're having a school concert tonight at the Church Hall.'

The town of Moorford, feeling the urge for economy, had decreed that the street lamps should not be lit upon moonlight nights, and as this was officially a moonlight night, in spite of the heavy bank of clouds overshadowing all sign of the moon and the drizzle of rain which was falling, the lamps were dark, and it was impossible for Jim to see the outlines of the car.

As they came abreast of the bank he took out the key which opened the side door.

'Going to work, sir?'

'No, I'm going to get my coat,' said Jim. 'I'll probably overtake you.'

The inspector went on, and Jim entered and closed the door behind him.

The inspector passing glanced up and saw lights in the windows of the living-rooms above the bank, where Mr Stephen Sanderson had his headquarters. More than this, he noted a light in an interior room which he recognised as the assistant manager's private office.

He had not gone a dozen yards when he heard a shot, and turned. He listened, but there was no outcry. It was undoubtedly a shot. He was an old soldier and could not mistake the sound. He walked quickly back to the bank and peered over the green-painted sashes of the window and looked in. He saw a silhouette of a figure against the glass door of Sanderson's office and knocked.

Then he went round to the side door. It was ajar, though he had distinctly remembered hearing Bartholomew close it.

He flashed his lamp into the interior and walked in. There was a door on the left of the passage. He turned the handle and found himself in Jim Bartholomew's private office. This too was empty and the key had been left in the lock.

'Who is that?' called a voice.

'Inspector Brown – is anything wrong?'

'Come in, will you, inspector.'

The inspector crossed the room, opened the glass-panelled door that gave into Sanderson's office, and there he stopped.

Jim Bartholomew was kneeling on the floor, looking down upon a prostrate figure that lay stretched stiff and stark by the side

68

of the desk.

'Good God!' said he. 'Why, it's Mr Sanderson. Is he hurt?'

'He is dead,' said Jim dully, and looked at the revolver in his hand. 'My pistol killed him.'

'I heard the shot as I was unlocking my door,' said Jim, 'and ran in. There was nobody here.'

He got on his feet and walked to the door in Sanderson's room which opened on to the passage leading to the side door. That was unfastened.

'He went out this way,' said Jim. 'Get out into the street, Brown. I'll search the house. The man who did this can't be far away.'

But evidently the murderer had made his or her escape by the same passage as the two men had entered. The slayer of Sanderson was probably not half a dozen feet from the inspector when he had pushed open the door which the murderer had left ajar in his flight, but when the inspector reached the street it was empty Far down to the southern end of the town was a tiny speck of red light. It was the car that they had seen waiting on the opposite side of the street and which was now disappearing from view.

Jim's search of the room above gave nothing. It revealed only one fact, that two persons had been there. Sanderson had had a visitor. There were two empty coffee cups on the table and in the saucer of one of these was the end of a cigarette, the type which Sanderson smoked.

There was no other clue, and he went back to the office and bent over the dead man. Sanderson had been shot at short range. Death must have come painlessly, for upon his face, now dignified by the Great Visitation, was a strange serenity and something of that good humour in which Jim had found him during the afternoon.

One hand of the dead man lay flat and open, turned downward on the floor, the other was tightly clenched. Jim lifted this. Between finger and thumb was a little slip of paper. He prised the fingers apart and took out the thing which Sanderson had been holding, carrying it to the table under the light. It was a torn portion of a photograph, and the untorn edges were about an inch and a half in length. The face, whatever face it was, had gone, but the one hand which showed was obviously the hand of a woman. Jim looked, and suddenly the room went round and round and he gripped the edge of the table for support, for upon the finger of that hand, the hand of this unknown woman, was the ring, the only one of its kind in the world, and there leered up to him with microscopic exactness the three dire faces of the Furies, the Daughters of the Night.

Mrs Cameron!

Whoever had killed Sanderson had killed him to steal that picture. Where had it come from? Then in a flash Jim remembered the package of photographs which had come from the District Attorney.

And Mrs Cameron's horror at the sight of him, and her change of plans ... the getting out at the Halt when she was supposed to be on her way to Scotland. He sat heavily on a chair, his head on his hands, shaking and ill.

He heard the thud of heavy feet in the passage, thrust the torn corner of the photograph in his waistcoat pocket, and got up to meet the inspector, who was unaccompanied.

'I'll have to fetch the doctor myself, Mr Bartholomew,' he said. 'The police doctor is out of town and I shall have to go up to Dr Grey at Oldshot. Will you wait?'

Jim nodded. He welcomed the interval. He wanted to think.

It was half an hour before the inspector returned accompanied by a doctor and another constable he had picked up on his beat. And a further surprise awaited him. The door was ajar but Jim Bartholomew had gone. On the table of the room where the murdered man was lying was a sheet of paper and a key and written upon the paper were the words:

'Telegraph to our bank at Tiverton to send a manager over to take charge. Give him this key.'

The inspector stared at the doctor and from the doctor to the constable.

'I don't understand it,' he said in a worried voice. 'Why did Mr Bartholomew go? And where has he gone?'

Information on both subjects was forthcoming. At two o'clock it was reported to the inspector that Mr Bartholomew had mounted the last train for Exeter as it was moving out of the station. At ten o'clock next morning in answer to the inspector's urgent wire arrived an official of the bank, who made a hasty inspection of the strongroom.

He came with a little disordered bundle in his hand and put it on the table, then consulted a deposit book.

'Deposit No. 64,' he read slowly, 'one dog collar of diamonds, property of Mrs Stella Markham of Tor Towers. Deposited at the bank on the 19th September. Valued £112,000 and insured by the bank. Premium paid.'

He looked from the book to the torn package. The seals had been ripped, the tapes broken, and the brown paper torn. Inside was a glass box – and it was empty.

That afternoon a warrant was issued for the arrest of James Bartholomew on a charge of murder and robbery. His description was telegraphed throughout the country and the busy radio sent forth urgent inquiries to all steamships which had left port that day and received the reply. 'Not aboard.'

6

Margot Cameron, leaning over the rail of the huge *Ceramia*, had watched the quay anxiously for some sign of Jim. He had promised to see her off and she knew that it must be some extraordinary circumstance which would keep him away. There was so much that she wanted to tell him, so much that she had forgotten to say when they had parted, and she could have wept when the clanging bell warned non-passengers to leave the ship.

She was still on the deck as the big liner swung into Southampton Waters, hoping that at the eleventh hour she would see him, and it was not until the ship was passing Netley that she went below with a sigh, to the luxurious suite which her brother had reserved.

The vastness of the apartments, their horrible emptiness, served to emphasise her loneliness, and for the first time in her life she felt genuinely homesick and could have cried. She shook off this weakness, changed her dress, took a book and went on the deck to find her chair.

Frank had made his arrangements very thoroughly and three chairs had been reserved amidships. A steward brought her rugs and pillow, and she settled down to get over what is invariably the most trying part of a voyage.

A fluttering label to one of the chairs caught her eye. She reached out and held it steadily.

'Mrs Dupreid' she read, and remembered that Cecile's friend was on board.

She put down her book and went down to the purser's office.

'Mrs Dupreid,' said one of the assistants. 'Yes, madam, she is in Stateroom 209, C Deck.'

Margot thanked him and went up the elevator to C Deck and began her search.

Stateroom 209 was amidships and she knocked at the door. A maid appeared.

'Is Mrs Dupreid in her cabin?' asked Margo.

'Yes, madam,' said the maid, 'but she doesn't want to see anybody.'

'Will you tell her it is Miss Cameron.'

'She knows you are on board, madam,' said the maid, 'and she told me to ask you to excuse her. She is feeling very unwell and she is not fit to see anybody.'

Margot was a little piqued by the uncompromising refusal, and with a conventional expression of regret she went back to her book on the promenade. The passengers had come up from lunch (she only realised then that in her anxiety to see Jim Bartholomew she had missed that rather important meal) and were taking up their chairs. Her own chair was the end of the four and next to her a steward was arranging cushions and soft fleecy rugs for a tall slim girl who stood watching the preparation without interest.

Margot glanced at her curiously. Women are always fascinating to other women, and somehow Margot sensed rather than knew the identity of her left-hand neighbour.

She was very pretty, about twenty-eight, Margot judged, with a spiritual face and dark deep eyes that seemed to Margot to look through and through her when they rested for a moment in her direction.

Presently the steward finished and the lady with a word of thanks seated herself.

Margot noticed that she was beautifully dressed and read too the title of her book, which was a book of reminiscences of a former police chief in New York. The lady did not read. Instead, to Margot's surprise, she turned to her.

'You're Miss Cameron, aren't you?' she asked.

'Yes,' smiled Margot, laying down her book.

'I heard that you were on board with your brother and his wife. I am a neighbour of yours. My name is Stella Markham.'

'Oh yes, I have seen your house. It was pointed out to me only a few days ago.' ('Designed for an emperor's palace or a lunatic asylum,' she remembered Jim's description.)

She shrugged (mentally) at the recollection, for she was not feeling too kindly about Jim. She had counted on his coming to see her off and he had failed her, had not even sent her a wire.

'Your brother and his wife are with you – yes?'

'Mr and Mrs Cameron aren't on board,' said Margot. 'They changed their plans at the last moment.'

'It is going to be a lonely voyage for you,' said Stella Markham, with a quiet smile.

'I prefer it so, I think,' replied Margot.

The conversation dropped hereabouts and

they both took up their books.

It was Stella Markham who broke the silence.

'Your sister-in-law was one of the two people I wanted to meet,' she said. 'Three if I include you,' she added with tact, and Margot laughed.

'Who was the other?' she asked, and was quite unprepared for the reply.

'I wanted to meet a bank manager there, a man named Bartholomew. And since I have been on board I have wanted to meet him more than ever.'

'But why?' asked the girl in surprise, praying that Mrs Stella Markham with the penetrating eyes would not observe her change of colour.

'I am told he is rather amusing,' drawled the girl, and Margot bridled. 'I am sitting at the table of the chief officer, Mr Stornoway, and he spoke about Mr Bartholomew when he heard I had come from Moorford.'

Margot remembered that Stornoway was one of the ship's officers whom Jim had mentioned.

'My dear,' Mrs Markham went on, 'he raved when I mentioned his name, though at first I thought he looked a little embarrassed. It appears that Mr Bartholomew was on a ship when it sunk and they were in the water for twelve hours, and if it hadn't been for our bank manager they would have both been drowned – he and another man who is also on this ship.'

'I have heard about it,' said Margot.

'Do you know him?'

'Mr Bartholomew? Yes, I know him rather well.'

'And is he very amusing?'

'Do you mean does he stand on his head and sing comic songs?' asked Margot coldly.

'No, I mean is he interesting?'

'Oh, immensely,' said Margot shortly, and again they drifted to their books, and again it was Mrs Markham who spoke.

'I am the dullest person in the world,' she said. 'I am bored, bored, bored, until I can find nothing in existence which justifies my living. I hate England and I hate America. I hate Paris worst of all.'

'Have you ever tried Coney Island?' asked Margot, who was beginning to dislike her languid companion. 'I am told that is rather amusing.'

The lady stiffened a little.

'I have never met anybody who has ever been to Coney Island,' she said, and went back to her book.

Margot took a turn up and down the deck by herself, then went down in the elevator to F Deck on which the purser's office was situated. Her conversation with Mrs Markham had reminded her that there was a possibility that Jim had sent a telegram after all. At any rate there would be one from her brother and sister. There was a wire from Frank, but none from Jim. Nor was there any message from Cecile. Margot remembered, however, that Cecile would be *en route* to Scotland and must find a difficulty in wiring in time to catch the boat.

She wandered aimlessly about the ship until teatime. There seemed to be nobody she knew on board, and in sheer ennui she went back to her cabin and lay down. She was aroused by the entry of her maid, who began setting out her dress for dinner.

'What time is it?'

'Half-past six, madam,' said the faithful Jenny, who looked pale and hollow-eyed.

'Have you been ill?' asked the girl.

'Yes, miss.'

'Then you're a silly goop,' said Margot cheerfully. 'The sea is like glass. Where are we?'

'We're near Cherbourg, madam. We arrive in an hour's time.'

The *Ceramia* called at Cherbourg for passengers and generally there was a stay of several hours.

Margot went into the restaurant to dinner. She had exchanged the table for three which Frank had booked for a table in one corner of the beautiful saloon and from her isolation scrutinised the restaurant without, however, finding anybody she knew very well. On the far side she caught a glimpse of Mrs Stella Markham wonderfully arrayed in black and heliotrope and she also was dining in solitary state.

Margot had her coffee in the big social hall, that seventh wonder of the maritime world, and listened to the band, and at eleven o'clock as the *Ceramia* was turning to leave Cherbourg she went to her suite for the night.

She was an excellent sailor, and though the ship took a roll in the swell of the English Channel she slept soundly till Jenny brought her morning coffee and rolls.

'There is no news for me, is there?'

'No, miss,' said Jenny.

'No wireless?'

'No, miss.'

'All right, put my bath ready.'

She was bitterly disappointed. If he could

not have come to see her, he could at least have sent her a message. Surely he knew, of course he knew, he who had been a sailor, that it was possible to communicate with people at sea.

When she was dressed she sought out the purser, with whom she had travelled before, and asked him a question.

'Oh yes, we're far enough away to get messages,' he said. 'As a matter of fact we've had several radios in the night.' He looked round and lowered his voice. 'One of which was an inquiry for a suspected murderer, by the way.'

7

Margot Cameron shivered.

'Is he on board?' she asked.

He laughed.

'No, no. They got me out of my bed about three to identify the gentleman and that meant going through about six hundred passports. Which annoyed me.'

The girl laughed in sympathy.

'Have you many passengers?'

'We're full up,' he said, 'and if I hadn't got the passports I couldn't have given them any answer at all – I certainly shouldn't parade the passengers in the middle of the night. As it was I was able to say that the man they seek is not on board. If he has left England, which is unlikely, he could have gone on a dozen ships. Saturday is a great sailing day. Be sure, Miss Cameron,' he said, 'I'll let you have any radio that comes within half an hour of its arrival.'

With that she had to be content. Church service relieved the tedium of the morning, and she dozed and read the weary hours away until nightfall. She saw Mrs Stella Markham again. It was difficult to avoid her, as her chair was next to Margot's and passengers retained the same chairs in the same positions throughout the voyage. They were sitting idling when an unhappy man waddled past and Mrs Markham laughed softly.

'That is my poor butler,' she said. 'He just loathes the sea.'

'Does he travel first class?' asked the girl in surprise, for servants usually are accommodated in the second saloon.

Mrs Markham nodded.

'Yes, why not?' she said coolly. 'If I had a dog he should go first class. I loathe second class people and I don't think third class people ought to live.'

'You're evidently a democrat,' said Margot politely, and the lady stared at her.

'I loathe people who are ironical and sarcastic,' she said.

'Then you loathe me most intensely,' laughed Margot, and a smile dawned at the corner of Stella Markham's straight lips.

'No, I don't exactly,' she said. 'You're so young and refreshing and I would give exactly two millions to change places with you.'

'Give who?' asked Margot quietly

'Oh, I forgot,' said Mrs Markham, and again the smile fluttered. 'Money doesn't mean a great deal to you. You're a lucky young lady.'

Just as she was going down to dress for dinner Margot remembered with a pang of remorse that she had not made inquiries of Mrs Dupreid and she went to her suite. Again the hard-faced maid met her.

'Mrs Dupreid is better and she is sleeping, madam,' she said. 'I take her on the deck at night for a little exercise.'

Margot came away with the sense that she had at least done her duty. The day never seemed to end and was like all second days at sea, interminable, and with a sigh of relief she got into her pyjamas that night and marked off the Sunday on her calendar, as a day nearer relief.

Monday was a replica of Sunday save that the weather had grown warmer and the passengers had discarded even their lightest overcoats and were leaning over the side or lying full stretched in their chairs on the sun deck basking in the bright sun.

There was nothing that promised the sensational developments which marked its close. Mrs Stella Markham gave her the first hint of unusual happenings.

'I had quite an exciting adventure last night,' she said, as she sat down by Margot's side.

'That sounds thrilling,' said Margot. 'And just now I want to be thrilled.'

'My cabin is on A Deck, that is to say on this promenade deck,' said Mrs Markham, 'and my windows open on to that portion of the promenade which is underneath the captain's bridge. It is rather an embarrassing position if one forgets to put up the shaded glass and even more embarrassing when loving couples linger outside after the lights are lowered at night – I think love talk is the most puerile in the world, don't you?'

'I don't know,' said Margot quietly; 'I have not had an opportunity of hearing it.'

The other looked at her and smiled.

'Well, the first adventure happened when I was on deck immediately after dinner. My maid went for a walk on the forward deck. Maids are rather a responsibility, especially if they get friendly with the men passengers. She was leaning over the rail looking at the third class people in the well deck when she saw somebody in my room. My bedroom is that nearest where she stood. It opens into a sitting-room and into a bathroom. She looked round and to her amazement she saw a woman peering into the room very timidly.'

'What kind of woman?'

'Well, that is where the girl's description breaks down. According to my maid, she was "heavily veiled," which sounds romantic but isn't very descriptive. I haven't seen any very heavily veiled passengers on the ship, though there are a few who might with advantage spare us the sight of their unpleasant faces.'

'What happened then?' asked Margot.

'The woman evidently saw my girl looking in and turned away quickly The girl ran round as fast as she could to the saloon entrance but there was no sign of woman veiled or otherwise and the cabins were empty.'

'Probably a passenger who made a mistake.'

'I thought of that,' said Mrs Markham, with a nod, 'but the most extraordinary thing is yet to come. About half-past eleven I took my final walk on the deck with Mr Winter – that is my butler, a very respectable man – and the Rev. Mr Price from Texas. We were talking about – various trivialities – you know the sort of conversation you can develop on a ship, and really a minister is the only third possible when one's butler is the second. And this sort of conversation went on until eight bells rang, which is midnight, and I said good night to Mr Price and we went back to my cabin. Winter always makes a point of seeing me into my cabin at night.

'When I got to my door and opened it I was surprised to find the lights turned on. I was about to remark upon the fact to Winter when a hand, a grimy hand, and a blue sleeve came round the open doorway from my bedroom, seized the switch and turned off the current. Mr Winter, in spite of his appearance, is a very courageous man and immediately ran into the room, switched on the light and dashed into my bedroom, which was in darkness. Just as he did so he saw a man slip through the window on to the foredeck like an eel, disappear over the rail of the deck down on to the well deck and out of sight.'

'Good heavens!' said the girl in alarm. 'Who was it?'

'He is a sailor – one of the ship's sailors, and, of course, I've made a complaint to the captain.'

'What was his object, do you think? Robbery?' asked Margot.

Mrs Markham nodded.

'I'm very careless with my small pieces of jewellery,' she said, 'and there was quite a number lying about, but evidently we must have disturbed him, for nothing was missing.'

'Did you see his face?'

'It was impossible for me, but Mr Winter said that the man was obviously a stoker. His face and his hands were black and he wore the blue dungarees which stokers on these oil-driven ships wear.'

Apparently the captain took a very serious view of the circumstances, for that afternoon all the stokers of the ship were paraded on the afterdeck and the sedate Mr Winter accompanied his mistress in an attempt to pick out the miscreant.

In this, however, he failed – the nearest he got being to identify the man who was on duty at the moment the visitation occurred.

At dinner that night the passengers were supplied with printed copies of the *Ceramia* bulletin, a little newspaper printed on the ship giving a summary of the world's news which had been received by wireless. Margot wondered whether there would be any reference to Mrs Markham's adventure.

The girl read the little paper carefully, but

in the main it consisted of extracts from speeches delivered by unimportant people upon subjects which were age-old. There was the result of the tennis championship, a few remarks upon the bank balances and the shifting exchanges, and that was all.

Margot was talking to the purser on the upper deck that night when Mrs Markham strolled up.

'Your bulletin isn't very interesting, Mr Purser,' she said.

'It is as interesting as we can make it, madam,' he answered, with a smile. 'You see we can only take the news they send us.'

'Was there nothing else crowded out?' she asked.

'Nothing at all, madam,' replied the purser. 'Were you expecting anything?'

'No, no,' she replied, with a shrug of her shoulder. 'Only one pines for something more exciting than Mr Balfour's views on popular education.'

As she walked away the purser looked after her.

'Has Mrs Markham told you what happened last night?'

Margot nodded.

'I wish it hadn't happened,' said the purser in a troubled voice. 'My work is quite hard enough without these wretched robberies or attempted robberies. There is generally something of the sort every voyage. When you get three thousand people in one hull it is any odds against your excluding a sprinkling of the criminal classes. Our own men on the ship are very honest. They've been with us for years and we've never had a complaint. Of course in the old days, with the stokers, we took on the scum of the earth, but now in the oil-burning ships we have our pick of the men and generally they are known personally to the chief engineer.'

'Mr Smythe?' she said.

'Yes, do you know him?'

'I know of him,' said the girl; 'he is a friend of a friend of mine.'

She was unusually wakeful that night and sat on the deck long after the majority of the strollers had gone below, reading under a bulkhead light.

She saw Mrs Markham leaning on the arm of her faithful butler, taking her final constitutional, and presently these two disappeared. Most of the lights on the ship had been extinguished, leaving bulkhead lights at rare intervals to furnish illumination for the late promenaders.

She was making up her mind to go below

when she saw a man walking slowly from the after end of the ship. He was in evening dress and he kept close to the rail, turning now and again to look upon the darkened waters. It was not until he came abreast of her that he turned his face and then she leapt up with a startled cry.

It was Jim Bartholomew!

8

'Jim!' she gasped, and put out both her hands. 'Why – why–'

'Ssh!' he said in a low voice. 'Don't call me Jim.'

'I don't understand.'

'Call me John Wilkinson,' he said, 'that seems a fairly good name.'

'But Jim, what has happened? What does it mean? Why are you on the ship? It's delightful. I was so worried about your not coming.'

He looked around.

'Walk to the rail,' he said, 'lean over and I'll talk to you. Margot' – his voice was low and serious – 'I want you to be a real friend of mine.'

'You need not ask me to be that,' she said. She was trembling with excitement.

'I am going to make a bigger demand on your patience than any man has made upon a woman before, I think,' he went on. 'First I want you to meet me here every night.'

'But why can't I see you in the daytime?'

'Because,' he said, 'there are reasons which, thank God! you don't know.'

Her heart was beating wildly, she was afraid, afraid for him. A thousand wild speculations passed through her mind and she was no nearer the solution of the mystery.

'I don't understand it,' she said, and laid her hand upon his, 'but I trust you and you're on board, and that's wonderful. What did you say your name is?'

'John Wilkinson. Frightfully unoriginal, but it is the first that came into my head.'

'Where is your cabin?'

He chuckled.

'I haven't a cabin,' he said, 'at least not to myself.'

'But, Jim—'

He squeezed her hand tight.

'Dear,' he said, 'four days ago I could have asked you to be my wife. I could have taken you in my arms and you would have been mine, but I missed my chance. A kind of vanity, which men call pride, would not allow me to ask you because you had money and I had little, and today it seems that I am not only in danger of losing you but of breaking your heart, unless you keep steadfast and have faith in me and I, by the grace of God, can make good in the next four days.'

'In the next four days?' she repeated.

He nodded.

'It seems strange, I who have talked about waiting for years to win out. I've got to make good in four days or I'm lost and finished. Now will you have that faith in me, Margot darling, and believe in me?'

She nodded, snuggling up against him.

'Now go below, dear, I'll stay where I am. There is a lynx-eyed ship's inspector coming along and I do not desire his company. Good night.'

He pulled one of her hands underneath his arm and kissed the fingertips. Margot went below, a little delirious, for all that was not joy was fear, fear for the man she loved and whose danger she knew was imminent.

The next morning she made a request of the chief steward which resulted in her being transferred from her loneliness to a seat at the purser's table. There were three other passengers, two of whom made no appearance during the voyage, and a third, a little German-American who had generally eaten his meal before Margot put in an appearance.

'I never had such a table,' said the purser in despair. 'I can tell you I'm awfully grateful to you for joining me, Miss Cameron.

You are making life worth living. In future every passenger who asks for a seat at my table must furnish me with a written guarantee that he will not miss a meal,' he laughed. 'In point of fact I've given another seat at the table to an Italian officer. Have you noticed him?'

'The man with the baggy riding breeches?' said the girl.

'That's the fellow,' said the purser. 'I think he must sleep in them.'

She had seen the dapper Italian staff officer, resplendent in grey and gold, had duly admired his polished riding boots, the generous proportions of his breeches, and the faultless cut of his high collared tunic.

'Visconti is his name, Pietro Visconti. He's an awful swell in Italy. One of the attachés to the Italian embassy, I believe. At any rate, he's travelling on a diplomatic passport.'

Soon after, the Italian officer made his appearance. He was a little, keen-faced man, very voluble, very polished, with a gift of bowing from his waist which was a little awe-inspiring. He spoke English fluently and would have fulfilled even Mrs Stella Markham's requirements in respect to his amusing qualities.

It was not necessary that Margot and he

should become good friends for Captain Pietro Visconti to confide in the girl in the afternoon that he was madly, passionately in love – with another lady, at which declaration Margot heaved a sigh of relief. The lady in question was none other than Mrs Markham, about whose eyes and stature and beauty, purity of complexion and grace of carriage, he spoke without comma or full stop for half an hour.

The girl was glad of the distraction, for if the days had seemed long before, this day was without end. She tried to sleep in the afternoon so that she might be fresh and bright for her interview with Jim that night, but sleep was denied her. It was on her return to the deck that she was the recipient of Captain Visconti's confidence.

Another distraction came in the evening when Mrs Markham introduced the Rev. Charles Price to her. Here she was agreeably surprised, for the Rev. Charles Price was a pleasant, well-read man who did not try to talk to her for her good and did not even reprove her when she lit a cigarette on the deck. Rather he held the match. He had been travelling in Europe for his health, he said.

'Nerves?' asked the girl quietly, and he was surprised.

'Yes. Why do you suggest that?' he said.

'Because you're still very jumpy,' she laughed. 'You have been looking round all the time you have been speaking to me and you start at every sound.'

He nodded.

'That's true,' he said. 'I think Mrs Markham's adventure has rather got on my nerves. I hate the thought of her, or of any woman, being liable to such an experience, though she is very plucky about it all.'

The steward was bringing round tea on little wicker trays and she shared her tray with Mr Price.

'I suppose you're going out to your friends?' he said, taking the tea she handed him.

'Well, I am in a way,' she replied. 'I am making a business visit, after which I'm going back to England – I hope.'

It occurred to her at that moment that there was no urgent hurry for her return. What Jim was going to do in New York she could not guess. Why he was there was beyond the wildest flights of her imagination. She remembered, as she had remembered a dozen times with a sinking of heart, that the next four days were vital to him. And where was he all this time? Why did he not appear

on deck with the other passengers, and what–
She gave it up with a little shrug of despair,
and Mr Price, who had been watching her
through his heavy-rimmed glasses, handed
back his empty cup.

'I think you want a little nerve cure
yourself, Miss Cameron,' he said.

At dinner that night she found in addition
to the bulletin a passenger list. She had been
wanting this and had not dared to ask for
one. She went carefully through the long
columns of names and came to the end with
a blank face.

Jim, was not there, either in his own name
or as John Wilkinson. She closed the
pamphlet thoughtfully and put it by the side
of her plate.

'Were you looking for anybody, Miss
Cameron?' asked the purser.

'Why – er – yes,' she said with as much
carelessness as she could assume; 'a friend
of mine said he might travel by this ship –
Mr Wilkinson, John Wilkinson?'

The purser shook his head.

'We haven't a Wilkinson aboard, either in
the first, second, or third class. I know that
because I had to go through the landing
tickets today and compare them with the
list.'

'Not on board?' she said incredulously.

He shook his head.

'No,' he said emphatically. 'We have no passengers by the name of Wilkinson, which is rather an unusual circumstance, because it is a fairly common name. But for the matter of that I once went three voyages without a Smith!'

He had to leave the table early for the pressure of work in the purser's department had been increased by the breakdown of his assistant.

'Oh, by the way, Miss Cameron,' he said as he was leaving, 'if you would like an un-usual experience tonight and you can keep awake so long, I will take you to the wireless room.'

Her eyes sparkled.

'I'd love that!' she said. 'But aren't you too busy?'

He shook his head.

'Even a purser is allowed time to sleep,' he said humorously. 'Could you be on the top deck at half-past twelve, and I will take you up.'

She had arranged to meet Jim and the interview was for twelve and it would be short. She nodded.

It was half-past eleven when she came on

the deck and at five minutes to twelve Jim came strolling along by the rail, pausing more frequently tonight to look out to sea because the weather was finer and the ship's motion was steadier and there were more passengers taking the air.

She walked down to meet him, noting that he had stopped between two bulkhead lights and leant over the rail. He was as correctly dressed as he had been on the previous night, but she thought his face looked a little peaky and worn.

'It has been rather hot today,' he said, when she asked him if he was not feeling well, 'and I have been – er – in my cabin.'

'Did you see Frank before you came away?'

He shook his head.

'I hadn't time,' he said. 'I didn't leave until Friday night.'

She did not ask him why, realising that that was tacitly forbidden.

'Margot,' he asked suddenly, 'will you tell me something about your sister-in-law?'

'Cecile,' she said in surprise.

He nodded.

'But, my dear, you know all there is to be known about her. She was married some seven years ago to Frank.'

'What was she before she was married?'

'What do you mean? She was well off. She was the daughter of Henrick Benson, who was a rich man and an artist. You remember he carved that ring which you called the Daughters of the Night.'

He nodded.

'Do you know anything else about the family?'

'Nothing, except that her sister, of whom she was very fond, had married unhappily when she was a girl of eighteen. I never heard very much about it because Cecile doesn't talk about those things. She ran away from college with a chauffeur or something, and naturally that isn't a thing Cecile would say much about. Anyway the poor girl died.'

'I know that,' said Jim. 'Do you know what became of her husband?'

The girl hesitated.

'Even that I am not certain about, but I have an idea that he was a pretty bad man and – and – went to prison for some crime. That is only an impression I have rather from what Cecile did not say than what she said. Magda's life was a tragedy – that was her name. Why do you ask me all this, Jim? No, no, I'm sorry. I've broken the rule.'

He leant toward her with a glance to left and right and kissed the tip of her ear.

'Pray hard for me, Margot. Pray like smoke for the next three days, for I am up against it good and hard.'

She pressed his arm.

'I do pray for you,' she said quietly.

'And have faith in me, whatever you hear.'

She nodded.

'Now go down below, dearie, and let me make a furtive way to my hiding place.'

She was leaving when he clutched her arm and drew her to the rail. Two passengers, young men, were strolling toward them talking. One she remembered having seen before, the other was a stranger. They were apparently ordinary first class passengers in the conventional garb of their class, but their appearance had a remarkable effect upon Jim.

'What is wrong?' she whispered as they passed. 'Do you know them?'

'One of 'em,' said Jim grimly. 'The fellow nearest to us – phew!'

'Who is he?'

He shook his head.

'I can guess,' he said quietly. 'The last time I saw him he was stripped to the waist and answered to the name of Nosey – on the whole I think it was a pretty good guess on the part of the man who named him. Go, dear, I must get away.'

When she went back to the deck again he was gone and the mysterious 'Nosey' had also disappeared.

She was joined soon after twelve by the purser, who showed her up the narrow gangway leading to the wireless room between the two giant smokestacks of the *Ceramia*. It was a hot little room, blazingly illuminated, for the valve lamps of the switchboard added to the glare of the overhead lights. The operator, a spectacled young man, explained to her the workings of the instruments, and presently she sat with earpieces clamped to her head listening delightedly to the shrill intermittent whine.

'That's the *Campania*,' explained the operator. 'She's three hundred miles astern.'

'How wonderful!' said the girl. 'And what is that other noise?'

He was lengthening the wave length, and 'the other noise' was a shrill almost imperceptible succession of sharp thin whistles.

'That is Aberdeen. It is the last you will hear from the old country,' he said. 'We shall be out of range tomorrow.'

One of the operators looked across.

'I expect that's the news coming through,' he said. 'Excuse me, miss. If you don't mind I'll take it down.'

He fastened the receivers to his ears and sat down, jerking an ebony key under his hand.

Presently he began to write. He looked round at the purser.

'I don't know whether it's worth while taking this down, sir,' he said; 'the chief officer said that no reference to the Moorford murder should appear in the bulletin?'

'Moorford – murder?' said the girl anxiously. 'Why, what was that?'

'Well, it's been censored out of the bulletin by the chief officer,' said the purser. 'I suppose he doesn't want to alarm the criminal in case he happens to be on board this ship. It happened at a bank.'

The girl stood with her back to the wall or she would have staggered. Her face was deathly white, but none noticed this in the fierce rays of the lamps.

'The assistant manager, a man named Stephenson, I think, or Sanderson, was shot dead, and the manager, Bartholomew, was found with a revolver in his hand. Apparently that could have been explained away, because Bartholomew had only left the police inspector a few minutes before, but that night Bartholomew disappeared taking with him a diamond necklace worth £112,000 which curiously enough is the property of a lady on this ship. We've just had a wireless through informing her of her loss and I'm delivering it in the morning.'

'What – what happened to Bartholomew?' asked the girl in a strangled voice.

'He got away,' said the purser, with a shrug. 'Clean away, apparently. Of course, they may have caught him since the last message came through. Is there anything in that?' he asked the operator.

'No, just a few extra bits of news. They have arrested a man in France, but it turns out that he is not Bartholomew.'

She took a step forward and would have fallen but for the support of the purser's arm.

9

'Why, Miss Cameron,' he said, with concern, 'I'm awfully sorry that I brought you here. Those lights are strong and the room is stifling.'

He led her out on to the boat deck on a level with which the wireless cabin was situated, and found a chair for her.

'Just wait here. I'll get you a glass of water,' he said, and hurried below.

A figure in the shadow of one of the boats moved and she saw the gleam of a white shirt front.

'Jim!' she whispered in agony. 'Jim!'

He crossed to her noiselessly and she saw that he was barefooted.

'Oh, Jim, I know! What does it mean? What does it mean?' she cried.

'You've heard?' he said quietly.

She could only nod.

'You have faith in me, Margot, haven't you?'

She drew a long breath and raised her eyes slowly to his.

'Yes, Jim. I have faith,' she said, and he bent down and held her for the space of a few seconds in his arms, his lips to hers.

The sound of the purser's boots on the brass-edged companionway sent him melting into the shadows.

'I'm better now,' she said, as she took the glass with a shaking hand.

'You don't look very much better,' said the purser. 'I can't tell you how sorry I am. I ought to have known that the room was too hot.'

'Oh, no, it's all right,' she said. 'It was my own fault, really. I – I had too much wine for dinner.'

'What a confession!' he said indignantly. 'You forget you sit at my table, Miss Cameron. Why, you haven't had wine since you've been on the ship.'

She laughed, but there was a note of hysteria in her laugh, and the purser was very glad to hand her to her maid.

Murder! Murder! The words rang in her ears as she tossed from side to side in her bed that night. The rush of the waters against the skin of the ship, the wail of the wind as it struck the scuttle of her open port, all seemed to carry the same burden of sound.

It was impossible. Jim couldn't have done

it. Jim, who used to talk mockingly of being a bank robber. It was absurd. It was tragic and yet here was a fact. There was a warrant against him and his flight confessed his guilt.

What could she do? She asked herself that question a thousand times and found no satisfactory answer. She could only have faith and wait, but where was Jim? In what part of the hold was he hiding? How could he escape the scrutiny of the inspectors who searched every yard of the ship twice a day for signs of stowaways, who examined the boats and penetrated into the noisome darkness of the ship's most secret places in search of unauthorised passengers?

She might ask these, and endless strings of other questions, and yet remain unsatisfied. It was nearly six o'clock before she dozed off, and the lunch bugle was sounded before she appeared on deck.

'I was wanting to see you,' it was Stella Markham who beckoned her. 'I've had some terrible news.'

Margot knew full well what that news was and at that moment she hated this languid, drawling woman as she had never hated any human being before. But for her wretched diamonds this crime would never have occurred. Why had she not taken them somewhere else? To London, or New York. She turned an inquiring face to the older woman.

'Yes?' she said, with an air of unconcern.

'I have lost a large dog collar of diamonds – stolen, my dear, by the bank manager,' said Mrs Markham. 'Of course, the bank will make good the loss because I am insured for them, but they were the finest stones–'

'Are you on the stage?' asked Margot rudely.

'My dear girl, no, why?'

'I thought only actresses lost diamonds worth £112,000 and dog collars made of the finest stones,' said the girl, exasperated beyond reason. 'Why do you leave them about or take them to banks; why don't you wear them and take all your own risks?'

The woman's thin eyebrows rose, and then she laughed.

'I forgot,' she said; 'it was the amusing bank manager who took them, and he was a friend of yours.'

'He still is a friend of mine,' flamed the girl.

'But how very interesting to know people of that class!' mocked Stella Markham.

'I don't know what you mean by that class,' the girl was in a cold fury. 'All I know is that your vanity and lack of forethought have brought about a good man's downfall' (Mrs Markham smiled indulgently) 'and a poor decent man's death.'

'Death?'

The smile vanished from Mrs Markham's face.

'Who is dead?' she asked quickly.

'Stephen Sanderson, the assistant manager. He was found shot dead in his office the night before we sailed.'

The woman's face went suddenly old.

'Mother of God!' she whispered. 'Shot dead! No, no!'

So terrible was the change in her appearance that Margot stepped up and caught her arm.

'Why, what is it?' she asked, but Mrs Markham made no reply.

She shook her head and then crumpled up back into her chair. She had fainted.

To Margot Cameron the memory of the days that followed seemed to her to be the memory of bad dreams. That night she was in her accustomed place to meet Jim, but Jim did not come. Earlier she had met the Rev.

Mr Price and Mrs Markham walking along the deck. Mrs Markham had fully recovered and was apologetic. At least she said she had fully recovered from her fainting fit, but the girl saw the dark rings round her eyes and drew her own conclusions.

'It is silly of me, but I never could hear of violent death without fainting,' she said, 'and it came as a double shock to me because I knew the poor man.'

'Mrs Markham has been telling me the sad news,' said Mr Price. 'It was terrible, terrible.'

He shook his head and there was conviction in his voice.

'That may account for–' began Mrs Markham.

'For what?' asked the gentleman when she paused.

'For what the deck steward told you this evening.'

'Oh yes,' said Mr Price, staring over the side of the ship.

'What was that?' asked the girl.

'The deck steward told me that there were two detectives on board. I cannot discover whether they are first class passengers.'

A new panic seized the girl.

'Detectives?' she said shakily. 'Who are

they? Could you point them out?'

'No,' said Mrs Markham, with a hint of irritation. 'Winter will probably know them, he's of that class of man who mixes with – detectives.'

'It is terrible!' said Mr Price again.

The story of the bank tragedy seemed to have affected him deeply.

'I – er – think I'll go to bed,' he said, 'if you ladies will excuse me.'

He turned abruptly and left them.

'I like that man,' said Margot. 'I don't know why but I think I like him.'

'Do you?' said Mrs Markham indifferently. 'Yes, he's quite a nice man, I should think.'

'Your man is not with you tonight.'

'He is under the weather,' said Mrs Markham brusquely. 'We had a head sea this morning and that was quite enough to put Mr Winter *hors de combat.*'

It was after this that Margot waited for Jim's appearance. She was still waiting when the watch came to hose the deck. She retired to her cabin that night and wept, almost for the first time in her life. She could not sleep, and at five o'clock when the dawn was showing through her porthole she got up, dressed herself, and went out on the deck.

The elevators were not running at that hour and she had to climb the broad companionway. When she reached C Deck she remembered Mrs Dupreid and smiled in spite of her sadness at the idea of calling on her at five o'clock in the morning.

Nevertheless she turned back and looked down the narrow passage which led to the stateroom.

Mrs Dupreid's cabin door was ajar and there was a light burning. Perhaps, thought Margot, she is as sleepless as I am, and after a moment's hesitation she went down the passage and knocked at the door.

At the knock the door swung open. The cabin was empty. What was more, the bed had not been slept in. Margot frowned. Probably Mrs Dupreid was on deck, and she climbed the remainder of the stairs and went out into the cold dawn.

The deck was empty save for a patrolling quartermaster who looked at her without interest, being inured to the eccentricities of passengers, but presently came back to her and asked her if she would like some coffee.

'I don't suppose any of the stewards are about so early, miss, but I can get you some if you wish.'

She gratefully accepted the offer.

He put a chair for her and covered it with a rug and she was beginning to enjoy the novelty of the experience.

The ship was rolling a little and she thought of Mr Winter sympathetically. A grey sea was running and the skies were lowering and promised rain.

'It will clear up before noon,' said the quartermaster in the way of all quarter-masters, whose lives are spent in explaining away bad weather to unhappy passengers. 'That's the greaser watch going on duty.'

A string of men was coming along the deck.

'They take a short cut in the morning when nobody's about.'

'What are greasers?'

'They're the fellows who look after the engines – stokers we used to call them – it's pretty hot, I can tell you, down below, with a temperature of 140. When they dragged a fellow out the other day it took two hours before he recovered consciousness!'

'Poor fellow!' said the girl. 'It is terrible that we people who live in such comfort do not realise what these men suffer.'

'Martha's Sons,' said the quartermaster profoundly, 'or Mary's sons, I ain't sure which. A chap wrote a poem once showing

115

that one lot of sons had to work for the other lot of sons.'

Margot nodded. The leader of the men was now abreast and they passed curious glances at her. She looked along the line and nearly dropped her cup.

It required all her self-possession to remain silent, for the seventh of the men, barefooted and bareheaded, looking straight ahead, was Jim Bartholomew, clad in stained blue jumper and ragged-ended trousers that did not come far below his knees.

10

He passed with the others at a jogtrot and left her speechless. The quartermaster was discussing with respectful fervour the inequalities of life and did not notice her agitation.

'Yes, miss, that's what it is. Some of us work in the engine room below and some of us sleep on the upper deck. But them as works in the engine room below have pleasures which the upper deck people know nothing about. There's many a man in the stokehole, miss,' he said impressively, 'who's as much of a gentleman as the best first class passenger that ever sailed. Think of 'em, miss, human beings, like you and me – loving–'

'Oh don't,' said the girl, putting out her hand.

'I'm sorry, miss,' said the quartermaster in surprise, and a little flattered that his eloquence had produced so remarkable a response.

'Will you get me another cup of coffee?

I'm afraid I've spilt this,' she said.

He took the cup and disappeared.

So that was it! That was the explanation of it all. Jim Bartholomew was a stoker! Then it came to her, in a flash. The chief engineer and the chief officer of the ship were his friends. It was the chief officer who suppressed the news of the murder. They had shipped him, taking all manners of risks for the sake of the man who had saved their lives at the risk of his own. And Jim was down there. She remembered the story of the man who had been dragged out and had been two hours in recovering and shuddered. He was down there at that moment. Well, it would be cool there in the early morning – cooler than in the heat of the day.

Then she recalled the mysterious 'Nosey' – 'The last time I saw him he was stripped to the waist.' Was he a stoker too? She had not seen the man since that night. But speculation here was brief. Her mind went back to Jim.

She made a brief calculation. If he went down at five he would come up at nine and probably not go on duty again until the afternoon. But the afternoon was the hottest and the purser had said that this was a hot ship, especially in the Gulf Stream. She wished that the man had not told her, and then repented of the wish. Perhaps that was the reason Jim had not come out to her that night.

In this she was nearly right. He had been on duty, toiling there in the bowels of this giant steamer and in an atmosphere which defied description. And he was doing it all for something, for someone. She knew that. It was not for himself. It was for – who else but for her?

She was smiling when the quartermaster brought her a fresh cup of coffee. She was smiling when she lay down upon her bed an hour later for a doze, and when she woke cramped and stiff, for she had not un-dressed, at three o'clock in the afternoon, her first thought was of Jim Bartholomew, a fugitive from justice, labouring in the stifling heat of the engine room and she laughed.

It was the laugh of pride, for she knew, none better, how terrible was his peril.

Memory brought another recollection of the early morning, her visit to the cabin of Mrs Dupreid. As soon as she was dressed she made her way to the stateroom of Cecile's friend and knocked at the door.

The same maid, who apparently spent

most of her time in the cabin, came in answer to the summons and whispered:

'Mrs Dupreid is asleep. She had a very bad night.'

'Indeed,' said Margot politely. 'What time did she go to bed?'

It was no business of hers, and it was impertinence to ask, as she knew.

'Oh, she went to bed before midnight, madam,' said the maid, and Margot went back to the deck puzzled.

Must there be a mystery about Mrs Dupreid, as well, she wondered? To Stella Markham she was more than ordinarily polite. This graceful creature had lost some of her poise in the last twenty-four hours. The undercurrent of insolence had gone from her tone and she was, as Margot told herself, more human than she had been before.

'Thank you, I had a very bad night,' she replied to the girl's inquiry. 'I hate this ship. There are times,' her voice was vibrant with passion, 'when I wish to God it were at the bottom of the sea!'

'Ask the captain, perhaps he'll sink it for you,' said Margot calmly. 'He has the reputation of being a most obliging man.'

The woman shot a glance at her, but her

obvious anger melted to a smile.

'It's childish of me to give way,' she said, 'and I stand properly rebuked. Phew! Isn't it hot?'

It was hot. The sea was like glass, for the quartermaster's promise of a break before noon had been miraculously fulfilled. Overhead the sky was an unflecked blue, and only patches of gulf weed stained the sapphire purity of the ocean.

'If it's hot here, I wonder what it is like in the engine room,' said Mrs Markham in her conversational tone. 'They tell me that one of the stokers, or greasers as they call them, died of apoplexy at midday. I asked the doctor going down to lunch, but of course he denied it. They never tell you the truth about these things on a ship.'

'I think this voyage is going to kill me too,' said Margot unsteadily, rising and walking to the rail.

Mrs Markham, who saw in this act nothing more than a piece of restlessness on the part of her companion, resumed the knitting which the arrival of Margot had interrupted.

Margot came back steeled to a further encounter. Somehow she knew that if it were true that a man had died, it could not be Jim.

'How is your butler?' she asked. 'Has he died of apoplexy?'

Mrs Markham went on knitting, her eyes fixed on her needles.

'No,' she said after a while. 'My butler is immortal.'

There was something in her tone which made the girl look at her.

'What do you mean?'

'I mean a good butler never dies,' said Mrs Markham.

Margot was looking up and down the deck.

'I never see him about.'

Mrs Markham shook her head.

'No, he keeps to the smoking-room. Here comes a friend of yours.'

'He is not my friend,' said Margot quickly, as the smirking Captain Pietro Visconti, resplendent in uniform, came marching along the deck.

'Queer little fellow,' said Mrs Markham, intent upon her work.

'Yes,' Margot added irreverently, 'he looks as though he has come straight from the hands of his Maker,' and the other laughed.

The dapper officer halted at the regulation pace, saluted punctiliously each of the ladies and shook hands solemnly with Margot.

'You were not down to lunch, miss,' he said. 'I am disconsolate. I promenade on this side, I promenade on the other side, but I do not see you. I climb to the boat deck and I promenade there also. I search in the social hall and in the palm court, but no, you are not there.'

Margot slipped away and left him with his divinity and hurried down to her friend the purser.

'I want you to be awfully kind to me, Mr Bray,' she said, when she found him alone in his office, sweltering in the heat, though the electric fans were going over his head.

'You may be sure that your wishes will be gratified, Miss Cameron,' he said gallantly.

'I want you to break one of the most cherished rules of the ship.'

'What is the most cherished rule of the ship?'

'Well, one is that you never give away secrets. You never tell us the number of knots you are going to run or what happens when the speed is reduced and why.'

He smiled.

'Sometimes we don't know in the purser's department.'

'Well, I am going to ask you.' It required an effort on her part and she had to swallow before she spoke. 'Is it true that a – a stoker died today?'

He looked grave.

'The story's out, is it? Yes, it is perfectly true. What do they say he died of?'

'They say heat apoplexy,' she said, her feet trembling beneath her.

'That isn't true. It was a blowout that killed him, poor chap. I am awfully sorry. He has been with the company for fifteen years.'

The girl drew a long sigh of relief which sounded like a sob.

'Thank you for telling me,' she said huskily. 'I wanted to know – something about it.'

'Why, Miss Cameron, one would think you had a friend in the stokehole,' he laughed, as he opened the door for her.

'They are all my friends in the stokehole,' she said. 'I am only just beginning to understand something of the burden which the Lord has laid upon the sons of Martha.' And the purser, who stood between Martha's sons and the pleasant-living sons of Mary, was silent.

The day had not been without adventure for Jim Bartholomew. His watch had been relieved and he was passing down the narrow alleyway communicating with his cramped quarters for'ard when somebody tapped him on the shoulder, and looking round he saw the greasy black face of the man beside whom he had been working that morning.

'I want to talk to you, Wilkinson,' said the stoker in a low voice. 'Turn into the bathroom.'

Jim obediently followed instructions.

The bathroom was a bare room fitted with showers and a long line of wash bowls and it was empty.

'What were you doing on the promenade deck last night?' asked the man called Nosey, and there was authority in his tone.

'I might ask the same question of you,' said Jim.

The other looked at him thoughtfully, then suddenly:

'Of course! You're Bartholomew!'

'That is a name,' said Jim, 'it is not necessarily mine.'

'Don't let us argue about that,' said the man; 'sit down somewhere – I'm dead tired, but I've got to have this thing out with you.'

They found two wooden stools.

'I'm going to tell you this,' said Nosey. 'I'm a Scotland Yard man, and though I'm not after you I have power to arrest you and will probably do so, though headquarters do not believe you committed the murder or stole the necklace – my pal, by the way, has a very full report by wireless of the affair. Now, the best thing you can do, Mr Bartholomew, is to tell me all you know and be perfectly frank. You won't have many opportunities, because I'm leaving the stokehole tomorrow or the next day – I'm satisfied that none of the people I want are in the ship's company.'

There was nothing to be gained by evasion or silence and Jim told everything to the last detail. For an hour they sat, the detective interrupting occasionally with a question, and at the end when they rose, the Scotland Yard man dropped his hand on the other's shoulder.

'There is somebody who is going to be pinched before this packet reaches the Hudson River – maybe it will be you.'

'I should hate you to go home empty-handed,' said Jim politely.

The routine of ship life had grown wearisome for Margot Cameron and she waited impatiently now, not for the hour of sleep, but the hour of meeting.

Once more she took her place by the rail on the darkest part of the deck that night, and Jim came along.

He was, as usual, in evening dress.

'You wonderful man!' she breathed and moved close to him. 'How is the work going? The big work, I mean.'

'I think it is going well,' he said.

He looked round.

'That infernal chief steward will see me, and he's the last man I want to meet, because unhappily he knows me. Will you turn boldly with me and compromise yourself for ever-lasting by coming to the boat deck unchaperoned.'

'I think I am compromised already,' said the girl, and slipped her arm into his.

The way up to the boat deck was by a narrow companion ladder, and she mounted first. There were one or two couples left, shadowy figures lying in their chairs, and the two moved for'ard, where the gangway is narrow and obstructed by bolts and stanchions.

Between two boats was a narrow platform from which the lowering was directed, and into one of these tiny alleyways they turned.

'Now I want you to tell me everything that has happened?' she said, and briefly he re-tailed all that happened up to the discovery of the body.

'I can't understand one thing,' she said.

'Why did Cecile get out at the Halt and go to her car, and why didn't you tell Frank?'

'Because I thought he knew,' said Jim. 'It puzzled me too. Did she say she was going to Scotland before she took her sudden decision?'

'No,' said the girl. 'It all came out in the talk she had with Frank in the study. It was a serious talk, because Frank looked very worried when he came out and poor Cecile looked positively ghastly. But you haven't told me all.'

'No, I haven't,' he said, and he did not speak for a while.

'There are two things. One I'll tell you and one I will keep until later. I will not tell you what happened after the inspector left me alone with the body. But this you shall know, and I want your help to solve the mystery. When I looked at poor Sanderson's hand I found that he was clutching a piece of paper. I prised his hand open and took out the corner of a photograph which had evidently been torn from his grasp.'

'A photograph of whom?' asked the girl quickly.

'Of nobody specially. It was just a corner, I tell you. All that was visible was a woman's hand.'

He was quiet.

'Yes,' said the girl.

'It was a hand, and on that hand,' said Jim, 'was a ring.'

The girl clutched his arm.

'Not the Daughters of the Night?' she asked in a whisper.

'Yes, the Daughters of the Night,' he said.

11

Cecile! Her ring – and yet–

'There was no doubt about it at all,' he said. 'Since I have been on the ship I have borrowed the chief engineer's magnifying glass and the enlargement shows clearly every detail of the carved faces.'

She was very silent and they stood leaning over the rail watching the water foaming at the ship's hull.

'Won't you tell me some more of what happened to yourself?'

'Only this,' he said. 'I arrived at Southampton at daybreak and went straight on board. I knew Smythe, the chief engineer, would be there and I explained frankly all that happened and told him my suspicions which I haven't given to you. He got Stornoway down to his cabin and we talked the matter over at lunch. Two wonderful fellows, they are! They took the risk. I berth in the chief engineer's cabin – which is on this deck, by the way,' he said. 'The steward is in the guilty secret, but he too is an old friend of mine.'

'What is going to happen in New York?'

'I don't know,' he said. 'There are detectives on the ship, but I hardly think that they are looking for me.'

'What are they here for?'

'They are after the Big Four. Did I tell you poor Sanderson's theory? Poor chap, almost the last thing he told me was the amount of reward that was offered for their arrest.'

'I don't know what to think,' said the girl after a while. 'The photograph of the ring stuns me. It is the only ring of its kind in the world. Frank has often said so. Oh, but it couldn't have been–' She could not finish the sentence and he did not attempt to finish it for her.

'Do you think that Cecile did this terrible thing?' she asked after a while.

'Shoot Sanderson. Good Lord, no!'

'Do you think she knew Sanderson? It almost seems as though she did. You remember how ill she became when she saw him from the car that day?'

He did not reply for a while, then:

'I should dismiss the possibility of your sister's guilt from your mind if I were you,' he said. 'I am perfectly convinced that she had no more to do with that murder than you or I.'

Suddenly from the darkness behind them rose a cry, a strangled cry like that of an animal. There was a scuttle of feet and the thud of something falling. At the first sound Jim had leapt into the darkness and the girl stumbled over him. She saw him bending over a dark object that lay against a bulkhead. He struck a match and looked down.

'Who is this gentleman?' he asked.

The girl looked over his shoulder, and shuddered at the sight of the blood that was trickling down the side of the unconscious man's head.

'Why, it's Mr Price,' she said, 'the clergyman.'

Evidently nobody aft had heard the cry, for they were left alone.

Jim lifted the stricken figure and propped him up with his back against the side of a raft. Presently the man groaned.

'How are you? Can you walk?' asked Jim.

At first he thought the man could not have recovered consciousness, for he did not make an immediate reply.

'I'll try,' said the voice, and with another groan he heaved himself on his feet with Jim's assistance.

'Terrible, terrible!' he muttered and repeated, 'terrible, terrible!'

'Are you better, Mr Price?' asked the girl.

'Yes, I'm better. Who is that?'

'It is Miss Cameron.'

'Very extraordinary, I fell over those bolts. It is so dark up here.'

'Who did this?' asked Jim.

'Did what?' demanded the other.

'Who hit you?' asked Jim again. 'You're not going to tell me you fell over a bolt, because I heard you struggling.' He struck another match. 'And somebody tried to strangle you, there's the marks round your throat!'

'I'm afraid you've been dreaming, sir,' said Price, 'but thank you for your kind attention,' and with this he staggered toward the companionway, holding on to the boats as he went.

'Humph!' said Jim. 'Well, that was fortunate.'

'Fortunate?' repeated the girl. 'Why fortunate?'

'Fortunate indeed,' said Jim, his voice shaking. 'I think you and I ought to be on our knees thanking God – at least I ought – and heaven knows I've got enough to be thankful for already.'

'Let's see where that cry came from.'

He went carefully along the narrow alleyways and stopped.

'Just about here, I think,' he said, 'almost opposite the entrance to the wireless room. Now let's go along and see the wireless gentleman.'

He passed through the narrow doorway and up a short flight of stairs to the 'public' office where passengers handed in their radios and where they were checked. There was a little pigeon-hole behind which sat an operator in his shirtsleeves.

'Did Mr Price take his change?' asked Jim suavely.

'Yes, sir, he took his change, one dollar and fifty cents.'

'I thought he gave you a ten-dollar bill,' said Jim at a random.

'That's just what he did do, sir, and the cable was eight dollars fifty cents,' said the operator patiently, and Jim thanked him.

'What does it mean?' asked the girl wonderingly when they were on the deck again.

'I wanted to know the length of the message and whether he sent a message at all. He sent a radio which cost him eight dollars fifty cents, which means that he sent about forty words, which is a fairly long message. He had sent that message and it was when he came out that they set upon him, and I should imagine that Mr Price is an extremely lucky man that he is not over the side of the ship.'

'Jim, there's one thing I want to ask you,' said the girl when he was taking leave of her. 'If things work out, as please God they will, and you are put right in the eyes of the world, are you – are you – how long will you–' She found it more difficult to frame her question than she had supposed.

'I will marry you just as soon as it is possible,' said Jim, 'even if I have to borrow the money from you to pay for the licence.'

12

Two more days. Today, tomorrow, and perhaps half another day was all that remained for Jim to put himself right. She did not doubt that he would win through, and yet the fear that he might not turned her cold. In the morning she was on deck immediately after breakfast and the first person she saw was Mr Price, sitting calmly in his chair reading a serious-looking volume. He touched his bandaged head to her in salute.

'I'm afraid I frightened you last night,' he said. 'It was very stupid of me to go wandering about the upper deck by myself.'

'I think if you had been by yourself you would have escaped injury,' she said.

He laughed, but his laugh ended with a little wince of pain.

'I see your young friend has convinced you that I was attacked by somebody. Believe me, my dear Miss Cameron, that is not so. Probably the cries you heard were some foolish young people skylarking on the other side of the deck. I have often heard them myself and have been similarly alarmed.'

'You were attacked, and anyway Mr – my friend did not say he heard you cry out,' she persisted, with a nod of her head; 'you were struck after sending a long radio message to New York.'

He dropped the book he was holding with a nervous start and looked at her between his half-closed eyes.

'You're not Miss Withers, by any chance?' he said in little more than a whisper.

She shook her head.

'Who is Miss Withers?' she demanded. 'Oh, I know, there's a woman detective. Mr' – it was only by biting her tongue that she could keep Jim Bartholomew's named unsaid – 'Mr Wilkinson told me that there was such a person.'

'Yes, there is a person named Withers, Agnes Withers I think her name is,' he said lazily. 'I seem to remember her figuring in a case and it must have been in her capacity as a detective. No, I meant another Miss Withers, an old friend of my – er – aunt.'

Captain Pietro Visconti came along just then and carried her off.

'I do not like that priest,' he said. 'I never did like priests.' He twirled his little moustaches thoughtfully. 'They are wolves in sheep's clothing. They are very bad for the young,' he smirked.

He was in a less emotional mood that morning, and sitting by her in Stella Markham's chair (Margot wondered whether he derived any extraordinary satisfaction from that association with the woman he so brazenly and openly worshipped) he talked about Italy and Milan his home; of his career in the army and during the war (she found afterwards that he had fought with distinction on the Tagliamento), and spoke so intimately of Washington that she asked him if he had been there before.

He nodded.

'Several times, but in a humble capacity, not as second attaché, to the greatest military nation on the earth.'

She smiled, and he reminded her gravely that the Romans had taught the world the art of war. He had to vacate his chair, for Stella Markham put in an appearance. The curious oldness which had come to her face, and which Margot had noticed two days before, had not entirely disappeared. She looked as if she had had no sleep and confirmed this impression with her first words.

'I saw the daybreak this morning,' she said.

'I've seen it one or two mornings,' laughed Margot. 'Can't you sleep?'

The woman shook her head.

'I haven't slept since I left Tor Towers,' she said, and raised her eyes. 'Great heavens, why did I ever leave there?'

'But you're going back, aren't you?'

'I suppose I shall be compelled to,' said Mrs Markham after a pause. 'I shall have to if there is any question of the insurance on my jewels – those which were stolen, you know. I have sent a radio to a firm of lawyers in London to watch my interests and I do not suppose there will be any very great difficulty. Well?'

It was Mr Winter, her butler, not as jovial or as rubicund as usual. He stood in a deferential attitude.

'There is a radio for you in your cabin, madam,' he said.

'All right, Winter.' She dismissed him with a nod. 'Even he is brightening up,' she explained. 'What has happened to Mr Price?'

She was standing a little ahead of the chairs and looking along the deck. She had seen the white bandage about the clergyman's head.

'Do you know, Miss Cameron?'

'Yes,' said the girl quietly. 'I think he met

with an accident last night on the boat deck.'

'An accident? I knew nothing about that.'

She walked along to Price and sat in a chair by his side for some time.

In the restless way of an ocean passenger Margot dropped her book and went walking. She picked up *en route* a little German-American who was her table companion. He was going back to America to marry and was very shy until she drew him out, then found him something of a rhapsodist.

She had made the second circuit of the deck and was approaching the spot where Mrs Markham sat talking to the clergyman when she saw the butler come from the companionway. He stood at some distance and waited until he caught Stella's eye. She rose and went downstairs, the butler following.

It was late in the afternoon before Margot saw Mrs Markham again. This time they met in the social hall where Margot was taking tea listening to the band, her heart and mind in the engine room below, for every thud of the screw reminded her of the man whose future was hanging by a thread.

Mrs Markham sailed in, radiantly beautiful to the girl's admiring eyes and wearing a dress of such design as turned a hundred pair of feminine eyes in her direction.

She pulled up an armchair to Margot's side.

'Where are you staying in New York?'

Margot gave her an address.

'I should like to see you there,' said Mrs Markham. 'I am going on to Richmond, but I shall be back in New York in a week or ten days.'

Insensibly Margot realised that Stella Markham's attitude had changed. From the light, almost patronising acquaintance, she had developed into a would-be friend. And her subsequent attitude supported Margot's theory. She talked of Devonshire, tried to get Margot to tell her something of their home life at Moor House, and expressed her regret that they had not met during their stay in England.

'I suppose you'll be met at New York?' she asked.

'Yes,' said Margot. 'I shall probably be met by my brother's lawyer – in fact, I think it is certain I shall be.'

'Who are his lawyers?' she asked interestedly. 'Mine are Peak and Jackson.'

'John B Rogers is Frank's lawyer. He used to be District Attorney.'

'I know him,' nodded Stella, 'at least I know him by repute. And everybody else, of course, knows him in New York.'

'Yes, I think he's rather popular.'

'I'm going on to Richmond immediately,' said Mrs Markham thoughtfully, 'and I brought a box of candies from Paris which I promised to give to a friend of mine the very day I landed.'

'Why not hand them to a messenger?'

'Because I don't know my friend's address. I told her to call for me at the very hotel you're staying at. I wonder if you would mind handing them to her and telling the clerk, if anybody inquires for me, to send her to you?'

'Not at all,' said the girl, with a smile.

It was one of those little commissions which she detested, but she thought that under the circumstances it would be ill-mannered to refuse.

'I will give you the candies before we leave the ship,' said Mrs Markham. 'Perhaps you will come down to my cabin – I've some lovely frocks I would like to show you. Why not come down this afternoon – now?'

Margot was curious to see Mrs Markham's cabin and accompanied her without hesitation. Her suite was at the fore end of

A Deck and consisted of two rooms, a bedroom and sitting room, the former of which was nearest the bow. It was a very pleasant cabin, though not in many respects as pleasant as Margot's own suite. The dresses that Stella Markham showed were beautiful and they alone were worth the visit. She was saying goodbye when Mrs Markham called her back.

'You might as well take these candies along now,' she said, and pulled a steel box from under the bed.

She tried the key in the lock and found some difficulty in inserting it. She held up the box and examined the keyhole closely.

'Somebody has been tampering with this,' she said, and again Margot saw that drawn look in her face.

After a while she succeeded in turning the key, lifted the lid and took out a flat circular package from which she stripped the wrappings, revealing a beautiful, satin-covered box, the top of which was hand-painted. This in turn she lifted and showed a layer of the most delicious-looking candies Margot had seen.

'You don't mind taking these, do you?' she asked.

'Not at all,' said Margot heartily, and

waited until the box was wrapped and tied about with string.

She carried the package back to her cabin and put it in her trunk. Stella Markham puzzled her. At first she thought she understood her perfectly, but every day presented some fresh phase, some new angle of the woman, and Margot felt her confidence in her own judgment shocked by the contradictions and irreconcilable phases of her character.

As she was stepping out of the elevator on the promenade deck Stella was waiting for her.

'I feel I must make this confession,' she said; 'there's a duty on sweets, and it struck me that if your friend the District Attorney sees you through the customs, he is so well known that nobody will bother you with an examination.'

Margot laughed.

'That idea had occurred to me,' she said.

Like every other day this was but a preparation for the night. To her the days began when she met her lover in the shadows of the boat deck and ended when they parted. All between was a weary interregnum relieved only by such excitements as chance brought to her. But of that excitement she was to have this day her fill. It began in the afternoon when she went into her cabin to find a not particularly agreeable odour of tobacco smoke.

She rang the bell for the stewardess.

'Who has been smoking in this suite?' she asked.

'Nobody, madam, that I know,' said the woman in surprise.

The girl sniffed around.

'I wouldn't mind if they smoked decent tobacco, but this is terrible stuff.'

She could not escape the impression that she had smelt that kind of tobacco before somewhere. She looked round the apartment and after a while she found what she was seeking, a little pile of cigar ash which had evidently been knocked off and had not broken in its fall.

She examined it carefully and then very thoughtfully went back to the deck. She saw Captain Pietro Visconti sitting by himself and she went straight to him.

'Captain Visconti,' she said, 'what were you doing in my suite this afternoon?'

He had jumped to his feet as she addressed him.

'In your suite, lady?' he said, with extravagant surprise. 'I have not been to your suite.'

She unwrapped the little paper and showed him the cigar ash, and he laughed.

'Ah, you are the Sherlock. You discover cigar ash, eh? Well, it is not mine. My cigars are peculiar.'

'Very peculiar,' she said emphatically.

'They are Italian,' he explained, 'but there are several people who smoke the same kind of cigars on this ship. I could find you a dozen. Why should I want to go into your room, Miss Cameron? I do not even know where it is.'

After such a flat denial she had to accept his statement and apologise. After all, he might have strolled in by accident. It was hardly likely that he would come furtively, smoking a cigar. And yet now she came to think of it, she had never seen him without a cigar, and once he had told her that he smoked them so unconsciously that he did not know whether they were between his teeth or not.

But if he came – why? Here was a problem she saved against her meeting Jim that night.

The second thrill came after dinner. It occurred to the girl that before the chocolates could be delivered it would be necessary to know the name of the person who would call for them, and as she was on the top deck she went down the alleyway to Mrs Markham's suite.

Mrs Markham was evidently in, for there was a light showing through the transom and she could hear the sound of voices. The girl knocked and at the same time turned the handle, never doubting that Stella Markham whom she had seen at dinner would be visible. To her surprise the door was locked. Presently she heard:

'Who is there?'

It was Stella Markham's voice which spoke, but the voice was so strange that she could hardly recognise her.

'It is I, Margot Cameron,' said the girl. 'I wanted to ask you something.'

'One moment.'

The light was suddenly switched out and the door was opened two inches. Yet even by the indifferent light that was left Margot saw that the woman's eyes were red with weeping.

'What is it, my dear?' asked Stella quietly.

'I wanted to know the name of the person who is to call for those candies.'

'I will tell you later, dear. Will you excuse me now?'

She shut the door almost in Margot's face

and again she heard the murmur of voices. The other person was evidently a woman and it was unlikely that it would be Stella's maid. If Margot had any doubt upon that subject it would have been set at rest when she saw the maid later on the fore part of the deck.

Who, then, was the visitor? Margot was not ordinarily curious, but she felt that it was her duty to collect information and in some indefinable way she was helping the cause of Jim Bartholomew by her efforts.

Instead of going back to the deck she went into the broad saloon entrance, from which the side alleyways gave, and after waiting half an hour she was rewarded by seeing a woman come out of Mrs Markham's cabin.

Instead of coming to the saloon entrance the visitor turned into one of the side alleys from which, as Margot knew, ran a smaller staircase to the lower deck. Instantly her mind was made up. She raced down the companionway to C Deck. She guessed rather than knew who the visitor was, and she was rewarded when she saw the tall black figure turn into Mrs Dupreid's cabin.

So it was Mrs Dupreid! Cecile's friend! Margot's head was in a whirl. She gave up trying to think consecutively. Jim would know. It was another problem for him. She relied upon him, believing that he already held the threads of the mystery in his hands.

The whole thing was beginning to bewilder her. Why did Mrs Dupreid visit Stella Markham, and why did Stella Markham weep? The thing was altogether too puzzling. She went to the quietest part of the ship, which was the library, and read one of Scott's novels and found in the artificiality of his unreal heroes and heroines something of calm.

At eleven o'clock the library lights were lowered as a general hint to all those who might still be enjoying its hospitality. There was another hour yet, but as they had agreed to meet on the upper deck there was no reason why Jim should not put in an appearance earlier. She blamed herself for not having suggested this, and, getting her cloak, she went on to the upper deck on the off chance of the same idea occurring to him.

This night the deck was deserted. There was a dance in the saloon below, which had attracted most of the younger people, and as she stepped cautiously along the obstructed way between the boats and the deckhouses she decided that it was just a little too lonely to wait alone and that if Jim was not there she would go down to the promenade again.

But Jim was there.

She stood stock still when she saw him. Dark as the night was, he was silhouetted clearly. He was standing by the rail at the end of the long boats – and Margot almost swooned, for there was a woman in his arms!

Margot stood as though paralysed. And yet there was no doubt. She could never mistake Jim Bartholomew, the set of his head and shoulders was inimitable.

It was Jim. He was whispering endearing words to his companion. She could hear the caress in his voice and the woman was crying. The girl held her head in her hands. Was she mad or dreaming? Was the ship filled with weeping women? She gasped. Was this Mrs Markham?

She must have made some sound, for suddenly the couple went apart and the woman melted into the darkness.

'Jim,' said Margot hoarsely.

'Yes, dear. I didn't expect you.'

'I guessed you didn't expect me,' she said quietly with a pathetic attempt at humour. 'Jim, who was that woman?'

He was silent.

'Who was that woman?'

'I can't tell you, dear.'

'Don't call me "dear,"' she said in a sudden fury. 'Jim, who was that woman? Will you tell me?'

'I can't tell you,' he said.

'Then I'll find out.' She swung on her heel and ran along the deck, indifferent to possible foot-traps, and was back in the saloon entrance, breathless but determined.

The first person she saw was Mrs Markham, who was talking to Visconti, waving a languid fan as she watched the dancing through the open door of the Social Hall. Margot went down the companionway at a run.

It was she!

She caught a glimpse of Mrs Dupreid's skirt as she disappeared into her cabin, and a minute later Margot was at the door knocking.

'Who is there?' said a muffled voice.

'It is Margot Cameron.'

'I'm sorry I cannot see you tonight. I am not well.'

'I am coming in to see you, Mrs Dupreid,' said the girl with determination. 'I am Margot Cameron, and Cecile is my sister-in-law.'

'You can't come in,' said the woman again, but Margot pressed aside all opposition, stepped into the cabin and slammed the door behind her.

'Now,' she said, and then – 'why why...! Cecile!'

It was Cecile Cameron, tear-stained and defiant, who faced her.

13

'Now, will you kindly tell me,' said Margot, sitting heavily down on the settee, 'what all this dam' mystery means?'

'Margot!' said Cecile.

'I know I am using violent language,' said Margot recklessly, 'but there is a time when respectability means stagnation. Will you kindly explain?'

'I can't,' said Cecile sadly; 'only I want you to know that Frank knows I'm here.'

'That's one comfort,' said Margot, a smile struggling in the corner of her lips, and the smile was one which was largely determined by her relief. 'So long as Frank knows you are here – how did you come here, by the way?'

'I decided to come on the boat and my friend Mrs Dupreid luckily was staying in North Devon. We were going to pick her up, if you remember, on the way to the boat.'

Margot nodded.

'I had a talk with Frank and I told him certain things and he agreed that it would be best perhaps if I went. Only I couldn't go under my own name for certain reasons. I wanted to be alone and I wanted to have the freedom to work as I wished to work. I saw Mrs Dupreid and she very kindly agreed to my plan, which was that I should take her passport and occupy her cabin and she would come on by a later boat. That is to say, when I can get the passport back to her.'

'That much I understand,' nodded Margot.

'But why are you here and why were you in Mrs Markham's cabin?'

Cecile shook her head.

'You've got to trust me, dear.'

'Oh yes, I'll trust you,' said Margot hopelessly. 'I've trusted Jim and I trust you, and tonight I had to trust you both together in the most compromising attitude, Cecile.'

'I had to howl to somebody,' said her sister-in-law 'I was surprised to meet him. You see, I take my little walks on the upper deck. I have to keep out of your way and I stumbled on him accidentally a night ago. We've been talking–' She hesitated.

'So I gather,' said Margot dryly, 'and rather a nice way of talking too. And really, dear old Cecile, I don't grudge Jim's sympathy a bit. Did he tell you that he himself is in need of quite a lot?'

'Yes,' said Cecile, nodding, 'poor boy.'

'And I hope you were sympathetic.'

'Of course I was,' said Cecile indignantly.

'And did he weep over you?' asked the remorseless Margot. 'One good weep deserves another.'

'I think sometimes, Margot, you're absolutely heartless. But darling, I'm so glad to see you,' she took the girl in her arms and squeezed her. 'It's been a perfect hell of a life–'

'Ssh!' reproved Margot. 'Now let's talk sensible. When am I to be let into this scandal?'

Cecile looked at her thoughtfully.

'Maybe the day we reach New York,' she said, 'that's if – if–'

'If what?'

'If things go well,' said Cecile guardedly.

'Do you know' – it was Margot's turn to hesitate – 'about the – the photograph?'

Cecile nodded.

'He told me everything.'

'Did you ever meet Mr Sanderson before?'

Cecile's back was toward the girl and she shook her head.

'Let that matter wait until we arrive, will you, dear, to please me?'

'To please you I'll do anything. I wonder if that Jim has waited for me?' she said, and went tearing out of the cabin.

An elevator was going up and she caught it, and arrived on the boat deck in time to whistle a disappearing figure.

'Oh, it's you, is it?' said Jim. 'Well, did you slay the lady?'

The girl shivered.

'Don't let's talk about slaying people,' she said. 'Cecile is a darling, of course, but she's a most mysterious and exasperating darling just now – and Jim, was it necessary that she should weep on your shirt front?'

'I couldn't very well take off my shirt,' said Jim calmly, and the girl smothered her laugh on his shoulder.

They snuggled together in the little place between the boats.

'When do you go back to your stokering?' asked the girl.

'Don't be frivolous about my stokering,' he said; 'it is a most unfrivolous occupation. Whilst you're here I am going to take you into my secret and if I do not tell you things that you want to know you must not ask me. You promise?'

'I promise,' she said.

'In the first place I want to tell you, as I have told you before and it was quite un- necessary to tell you ever, that I did not steal

Mrs Markham's jewels. That necklace was stolen by what poor Sanderson called The Big Four. It is pretty well confirmed, I think, that there is a Big Four – that is to say, a gang of four have been working together and have been engineering the big jewel robberies which have created such a sensation in Europe. It was a member of the Big Four who stole Mrs Markham's jewels.'

'Who are the Big Four?' she asked. 'Oh, I beg your pardon. Is that a forbidden question?'

'It is and it isn't,' he said. 'It is a forbidden question because it is one I cannot very easily answer. I can't answer it because I am not certain. We know that there are two people named Trenton, both of whom have served terms of imprisonment in the United States – Sanderson told me that. They are a man and a woman, and at this particular moment there are two detectives from Scotland Yard on board the ship who are searching very carefully amongst the second and third class passengers. The third of the four is a Spaniard named Antonio Romano. The fourth, and really the keystone of the arch, though he is not the leader – Trenton is that – is a man named Talbot who is an expert forger and has made the obtaining of jewels a special branch of his study. It is certain that two of the four are on board this ship. Scotland Yard has had information to that effect.'

'How do you know?'

'Because one of the Scotland Yard men works in my watch,' was the surprising reply.

'Is he a stoker?' asked the girl, then quickly, 'the man you call "Nosey"?'

'Yes. I guessed who he was that night on deck, and when he asked me if I was Jim Bartholomew, who was wanted for the murder–'

The girl went white.

'You didn't tell him that!' she said faintly. 'Oh, tell me you didn't say that!'

'Oh yes I did,' said Jim. 'Don't be silly, darling. You don't suppose I'm going to be in hiding all my life? If I can't clear up this mystery on the voyage, I am going back to stand my trial and prove conclusively that I neither shot Sanderson nor stole the jewels.'

He kissed her gently, and presently her panic feeling wore off.

'I shall be grey when this ship reaches port,' she said.

'And I shall be a deep oil-burnt red,' said Jim. 'Shall I go on?'

'Oh, do, please.'

'Well, there isn't any more to say,' he said disappointingly, 'and it will ease your mind to know that if I hadn't spoken to Sergeant Rawson, who is my companion in misery, I wouldn't have had a ghost of a chance of getting ashore in New York. When we anchor off Ellis Island there will be a young army of American detectives on board looking for the gang, and I think it is pretty certain they will find them.'

'Why?' asked the girl.

'Because one of them has turned States Evidence. He sent a radio to Washington on the night he was nearly killed?'

The girl would have cried out in her astonishment, but he put his hand over her mouth.

'Mr Price?' she whispered.

'Price, or Talbot, that is one of them. He is turning States Evidence and I'd have given anything to have seen the contents of his message. Talbot is a man who is going to do things, and he's the man who is going to restore to Mrs Markham her filched dog collar. And I hope she will let her dog wear it,' he added viciously.

'Poor darling,' she laughed. 'Do you know I feel ever so much better and happier. This has been a really wonderful voyage.'

'Hasn't it?' he said sardonically. 'If you could see how sunburnt I am from the waist' – he changed his tone – 'and yet it's worth it. I'd give twice the time in twice as difficult circumstances for this stolen hour with you.' Then suddenly, 'Let's go down on to the promenade deck and be bold.'

The deck was fairly clear of people and they walked up and down, talking of Devonshire, of America, of all things in the world save the thing that was in their hearts. At the end of the deck for'ard where it turned before the cabins on A Deck they saw 'Mr Price'. He was leaning over the rail, looking down at the deck below in a meditative and thoughtful way. About twenty yards away sitting in a chair under one of the bulkhead lights and smoking aimlessly was an exquisite young gentleman in immaculate evening kit. Margot recognised him as the passenger whom she had seen promenading with the man called 'Nosey.'

'Do you see that lad?' asked Jim as they passed him.

'Yes.'

'That is the other detective. He's engaged in watching Price, or Talbot, to see that the gang do not get him. They nearly got him the other night.'

'But what a fine time he has, compared with the man in the stokehole!' said the girl.

Jim chuckled.

'They tossed as to who should go first class and my friend lost,' he said.

They made a circuit of the deck three times and still Mr Price leant over the rail with his head sunk on his chest and his arms folded. The fourth time they came round Jim stopped before the young watcher.

'Our friend has been there some time, hasn't he?' he said.

The watcher dropped his cigarette and looked along the deck.

'Yes, he's been there for half an hour.'

'Has anybody been near him?'

Evidently the detective knew Jim. (The girl discovered later that the two policemen and Jim had had a conference that night in the chief engineer's cabin.)

'Nobody has been near him,' he said. 'Of course, lots of people have been walking past him like you and others.'

'I wonder what he's thinking about?' said Jim.

'Poor man,' said the girl pityingly.

'Well, Price ought to be happy,' replied the detective, with a laugh. 'He had a radio from the American Government today, saying that he will be pardoned and that his evidence will be accepted on behalf of the State.'

He strolled up toward the meditating figure, and laid his hand on his shoulder.

'Now, Mr Price,' he said. 'You ought to be going to bed, you know.'

Price did not reply, and the detective bent over and looked at him. Then he turned and strolled back, his hands in his pockets.

'I think, Miss Cameron,' he said, 'I think,' he said carefully, 'you ought to go downstairs to bed.'

Jim looked at him, and the girl looked at Jim and nodded.

'Is he – hurt?' she whispered.

'Oh no, but he has little fainting attacks,' said the detective. 'Fits, you know, and people hate being seen when they're like that.'

She accepted the lie as gospel and with a smile to Jim went down below.

Then Jim and the detective went forward and laid the dead man down on the deck and the detective pulled out the stiletto from his side.

14

Nothing keeps a secret so truly as a ship. For a ship's company, from captain to bellboy, are born conspirators against revelation. None of the passengers, save those immediately concerned, who sat down to breakfast the next morning knew or guessed the tragedy which had been enacted in the night.

Price's place at the table had been laid for him, his serviette folded on his left, his hot rolls and coffee were waiting for him at half-past eight, the hour at which he invariably took his first meal.

The deck steward dried the spray from his chair, put his cushion and books ready, though he in common with every other deck hand knew that somewhere down near the keel of the ship, in a little room devoid of light, Mr Price lay dead.

Margot knew so little that, discovering Mr Price's cabin, she sent down a message to ask how he was, and the steward, who at that moment was packing the murdered man's belongings, returned the message that he was a little better but was not coming on deck that day.

The bellboy who brought the message to her, the deck steward who heard it delivered, the very band as they broke into a march at their eleven o'clock performance were all well aware that at twelve o'clock the previous night a passenger had been murdered in cold blood – but the passengers knew nothing.

Mr Winter, the butler, was one of those who inquired for the Rev. Mr Price. He inquired of the smoke room steward. The smoke room steward, who not only knew that Mr Price was dead but had helped to carry his body below, replied that Mr Price had been in there a few moments before and had just gone out.

That day, which had opened so sunnily, was not fortunate from the point of view of the ship's run. Towards midday they ran into a dense white fog and for the rest of the day the *Ceramia* crawled forward at ten knots an hour, her siren blowing at deafening intervals. It was clammy and chilly on the promenades and the decks were so wet and slippery that even walking was uncomfortable. Nevertheless Margot maintained her chair and, enveloped in rugs, preferred the open air to the clearer atmosphere of her cabin. Not so Stella Markham, who retired to her own sitting-room.

Margot had spent the greater part of the morning with her sister-in-law, who had elected to remain in obscurity until the voyage was ended. She did, however, prevail upon Cecile to shift her cabin to the larger and more comfortable suite which Margot was occupying.

'I shall have you near me, but there are two entrances to the suite, so you can go in and out as you like. I only ask this, that if you decide to entertain Jim Bartholomew, you invite me to your party.'

Cecile smiled.

'You've never forgiven me, have you, Margot?'

'I've forgiven you because I have a Christian spirit,' said Margot. 'But I don't think that sort of thing ought to become a habit. If you want to weep, darling, you come along and weep on me. I'm ever so much less knobbly than Jim.'

The fog continued throughout the day, but cleared up in the evening, only to gather even more densely after dinner.

Margot had come to know the watches below which Jim was keeping and she knew that this was one of his early nights and there was a prospect of his getting on to the boat deck long before his usual hour. She simply sat and killed time with a book, wrapped up in her big rug cape, and Mrs Markham coming out on the deck with a face which expressed her disgust at the weather called her sanity into question.

'Ugh! It's beastly,' she said. 'I wonder if we shall run into an iceberg or anything?'

'You're a cheerful little soul,' said Margot. 'Have you ever been happy, Mrs Markham?'

To her surprise Stella Markham turned on her with a face that was haggard with fury.

'I don't think you know what happiness is if you ever think I've been happy, or you can trace any look of happiness in me, Margot,' she said. 'I've never been happy, I never shall be happy. How would you like to stand before your Maker and confess that much?'

Margot was silent. She saw the woman's bosom rise and fall in her agitation.

'I'm sorry,' she said gently. 'I didn't mean to be rude. I was just being funny.'

'Of course you were.' Mrs Markham's anger vanished and she dropped her hand upon the girl's shoulder. 'I'm just full of nerves tonight. I'm going back to that infernal cabin to read.'

Mrs Markham was sick of body and sick

of heart. True to her word she went straight back to her cabin and found Mr Winter waiting for her.

'You have the key, madam,' he said.

She took it out of her pocket, put it in the lock and opened the door. The place was in darkness. So also was her bedroom, and this she approached, switching on the light. She heard the movement of feet almost as her hand was on the electric switch. The man who stood with one hand upon the open window ready to spring was in evening dress, but the lower half of his face was covered by a handkerchief.

'Winter!' called Mrs Markham loudly, and the butler came in.

The masked man turned to face the levelled barrel of a revolver.

'What are you doing here?' asked Mrs Markham.

It was a question which was superfluous. Two drawers had been pulled out and their contents were strewn on one of the settees. The intruder had made no attempt to disguise his presence. The bed was rumpled as though the mattress had been pulled up and examined. A wardrobe was open and apparently the marauder had this time dispensed with the ordinary light, for he carried a small electric torch.

'Put up your hands,' said Mr Winter. 'Put them up, sir.'

With a quick movement of her hand Mrs Markham tore away the mask from Jim Bartholomew's face.

She nodded.

'I know you,' she said; 'you're a friend of Margot's.'

'Got me first time,' said Jim.

At first he had put up his hands before the menacing pistol, but now put them into his pockets.

'What are you doing here?'

Jim's eyes wandered from one confusion of effects to another as he smiled, and he had a particularly happy smile.

'That's a silly question to ask!' he said coolly. 'It must be pretty evident to you that I haven't been tidying up!'

'You've been looking for something, haven't you?'

'That's about the size of it,' said Jim. 'You can put your revolver away, Mr Winter. There is going to be no shooting.'

'I'm going to take you before the captain straight away,' said Winter. His face was pale, whether from fury or fear Jim did not trouble to consider.

'I don't think you will,' he said gently. 'After all, I can't run away from the ship. There's no necessity for disturbing the captain at this hour, even if they allow you to disturb him, which is extremely doubtful. You know me, you can find me when you want me.'

'Suppose we can't find you when we want you, Mr Bartholomew – I think that is your name?'

'That is my name,' said Jim.

There was an awkward pause.

'You can go,' said Stella Markham.

'You wouldn't like to search me before I went, I suppose,' said Jim.

'You can go,' she said again, pointing to the door. She was whiter of face than Winter.

'Wait,' it was Mr Winter who blocked the entrance. 'I don't think that is how it should be arranged, Mrs Markham.'

He was a strapping, strongly built man, but Jim pushed him aside as though he had been a child and walked past him on to A Deck.

He missed the girl and guessed that she was waiting for him up above, and there he found her. She had gone to her cabin and changed from her flimsy evening gown to a costume more suitable for a *téte-à-téte* on a foggy night.

'Tomorrow,' were his first words, 'I am going to be a respectable member of society. In other words, I am coming first class with my friend from Scotland Yard, who is just about as tired of stoking oil engines as I am.'

'What is going to happen?' asked Margot.

'Well,' he said, 'tomorrow evening we pass Fire Island Light and some time later we anchor off Sandy Hook. The next day the Federal authorities come aboard and we shall see what we shall see.'

The fog was thinning, but the ship was still keeping to her steady ten knots.

'You're a little tired tonight, aren't you?' she asked. 'You're not speaking.'

'I've had rather an exciting experience,' he said. 'I'll tell you about it one of these days. And also I am a little tired. This fog means extra duty in the stokehole. Everybody stands by and the watches are doubled.'

'Then I won't keep you,' she said dismally, and he caught her up in his arms.

'That's just what you were proposing to do a few days ago, and maybe what you'll have to do yet,' he said – 'that is, if I escape jail.'

'Really, I think I'll go down and go to bed. Good night, Jim.'

He kissed her again and watched her as she walked back toward the companion ladder. Then he turned and strolled in the opposite direction.

She was nearing the ladder when she remembered that she had not asked him about their next meeting and she turned back. When she saw him he was leaning over the rail where she had seen him with Cecile in his arms. He was more clearly silhouetted because the fog formed a white background for him, and she stood a moment watching him.

As she did so she saw a figure steal out of the shadow of the boats, saw something rise and fall, heard the horrible impact as it struck Jim and saw him droop limply over the rail. She tried to scream but she could not. Then before she could utter a word or move she saw Jim's assailant stoop and lift him by the legs, using the rail as a fulcrum.

Higher and higher – and then the girl screamed. But it was too late. As the black figure darted back into the darkness Jim toppled over the side and she heard the splash as he struck the water. She screamed again and raced down the alleyway toward the stern of the ship. Her mind was made up and when she came to the limit of the deck she jumped on the rails, ripped off her skirt and taking one look to locate the dark figure which showed in the light from the port-holes, she sprang, straight as an arrow, into the water.

It was not as chilly as she had expected and she came to the surface and looked round. She saw the dark bulk of Jim's shoulders and swam straight to him as he sank. Her arm was round him as the stern of the vessel cleared them. Then something struck the water with a splash and a vivid green flare burnt within three yards of her. She turned and saw the red lifebuoy with the spluttering calcium light and dragged Jim toward it. They had been seen, and even as she looked and saw the vast stern of the *Ceramia* towering above her, the liner turned sharply to starboard and suddenly the screws were still.

She heard voices on the deck and the creak of a boat being lowered and clung desperately to the lifebuoy. Jim had recovered consciousness but was still too dazed to afford much help. She hooked his arm into the buoy and kept treading water. Suppose the light failed? Suppose they could not find her in the darkness? Already the ship seemed miles away and she could not see the boat if they had lowered it, but the calcium light burnt in a continuous splutter and presently she heard the creaking of oars and the ship's lifeboat, looking monstrously large seen from that angle, came alongside.

15

They lifted Jim into the boat and the girl followed. She was attired only in blouse and petticoat, and it did not occur to her until the boat was hauled up to the level boat deck and then she was thankful for the mercy of darkness until somebody put a coat around her and she made her escape to her cabin.

She had a hot bath and changed, and then in spite of the protests of Cecile went out to discover what had happened to Jim. She found him dressed in tweeds, the centre of an interested circle of passengers and he was lying outrageously.

'I went to sleep and fell over the rails,' he said. 'Miss Cameron saw me – I don't remember anything until I recovered consciousness with the calcium light blazing and Miss Cameron holding me up by my ears.'

The quartermaster on watch aft had witnessed the fall and he it was who had thrown the lifebuoy. This Jim discovered later. The doctor had dressed his head and to Margot's relief the wound was not very serious. The man who struck it must have been nervous, for he did no more damage than a couple of stitches remedied.

'As for you,' said Jim when he was alone with her, 'I owe you something more–'

'I'll present my bill one of these days,' she interrupted hastily, 'and now I'm going back to my cabin – you seem quite your old talkative self,' and with a gentle squeeze of his arm, she was gone.

His head was racking the next morning when he woke. Accommodation had been found for him on F Deck and he shared a big cabin with the two men from Scotland Yard. The visit of the doctor, the application of a new dressing, and the swallowing of a draught reduced his agony to a mere irritation.

That morning Mr Winter attended the commander of the ship and tendered a complaint against the victim of the last night's adventure. His complaint was listened to respectfully and he was informed that the matter was already in the hands of the authorities. Whereupon Mr Winter in his animosity grew a little venomous for one so respectable and typically English.

'I suppose you know, sir.' he said, 'that this

man Bartholomew is a fugitive from justice and the police have a warrant out for him, on a charge of murder?'

'I know all about that,' said the commander politely. 'Are you a police officer?'

'No, sir, I am not,' said Mr Winter, with dignity.

'Well, there are police officers on the ship who are attending to that matter,' said the commander, 'and you can rest assured that they will not shirk their duty.'

Mrs Markham had chosen the time of Winter's appointment with the captain for an interview which she badly wanted. Visconti, idling about the deck as radiant and gorgeous a figure as ever, saw Stella come from the companionway and instantly obeyed her beckoning finger.

'Will you come down to my cabin, Captain Visconti?' she asked.

'Madam' – he bowed low – 'what would give me greater happiness?'

'I want to show you those Tanagra figures I bought in Italy last year,' she said carelessly and he followed her to the end of the alleyway and into her cabin.

She closed the door behind him and motioned him to a settee.

'Tony,' she said, almost wailed, 'Tony,

what was wrong? Oh, my God! Why did you kill Talbot?'

The Spaniard had set his kepi down on the seat beside him and did not raise his eyes from the floor.

'Had he–?' she began again.

'He had turned States Evidence,' said Tony.

'But how – when?'

The man she called Tony shrugged his elegant shoulders.

'He has been in a blue funk for a month past. You know that, madonna. I had to keep close to his side all the time he was in Paris and never let him out of my sight when he was in London. The discovery that there were detectives on board must have driven him into a panic, for two days after we sailed he sent a preliminary radio to Washington asking if evidence would be accepted from one of the gang and whether that member who betrayed the others would be treated favourably. On receipt of a reply he sent a longer wire – Winter saw him writing it and guessed what it was all about. Like a fool, too, Talbot had kept copies of his wires and Winter found them in his cabin.'

The woman was silent.

'Who are the detectives?' she asked. 'Do

you know them?'

He nodded.

'There is one who has been working in the stokehole with Bartholomew, and another who has been amongst the first class passengers all the voyage.'

'Are they after – us?'

He smiled.

'I don't know whether they're after you,' he said. 'I should think not. Talbot never suggested in his wire that you were on board.'

'But they will know,' she said, fretfully plucking at her dress, and he rose slowly to his feet, walked across to her and laid his hand upon her bowed shoulder.

'Madonna,' he said earnestly, 'there is a way out for you, unless Winter–' He stopped and bit his lip thoughtfully.

'What do you mean?' she asked, looking up quickly.

'I mean you cannot be associated with any of the jobs which we have done. That necklace business at Moorford – is that the name of the place?'

She nodded.

'Even that cannot be charged to you. Winter's job again. Why did he do that?' he asked suddenly. 'I always thought the diamonds were your own.'

She nodded again.

'The only honest money I ever made in my life,' she said bitterly. 'Somebody who – who was fond of me gave me an option on Eastern Lands and that was the profit. I put the money into diamonds because Winter advised me.'

'You were foolish,' said the other. 'I see now. Winter would not like you having independent means or money of your own and he threw your jewels into the stock. I have been interested in the fate of that necklace – today I am more happy about it.'

He looked down at her meditatively.

'Shall I tell you something, madonna?' he said more softly than he had spoken, and she looked up with alarm in her eyes.

'No, please do not.'

He gave one of his extravagant little gestures, but the hard brown eyes which had directed the stroke that ended the life of Talbot the forger were soft and humid.

'I love you greatly, madonna, and I know that is a very bad thing for you to hear, because I am a man who has done many terrible deeds, but I worship you as children worship God.' He paused and then went on slowly, 'I will do everything to keep you out of this if our voyage ends badly.'

'But Winter?' she asked, and the Spaniard who posed as an Italian showed his teeth in a smile which was not pleasant.

'I do not regret Talbot,' he went on as though speaking his thoughts aloud. 'I know the man and he was bad. If I have blood on my hands, so also has he. You do not remember the case of the girl Hien – no, that would be when you were in–'

The door opened violently and Winter came in and his face was livid with rage.

'Well,' he scowled at Tony, 'what do you want?' and Tony smiled.

'Civility from you, my good Winter,' he said lightly, 'and a more amiable cast of countenance.'

'Amiable?' snarled the other. 'Do you know that Fire Island Lightship is right ahead?'

'The proximity of lightships does not distress me any,' said Tony cheerfully. 'Indeed, in such foggy weather as this, it is a pleasure to know that there is a lightship in the neighbourhood.'

'See here, Tony, don't get fresh with me. Do you know what the lightship means to you and me?' asked Winter.

He had dropped his somewhat exaggerated English accent. His drawl and finicking intonation had gone and he snapped his words. There was a wicked look in his eyes as he towered above the dapper little man.

'Why should I not get fresh with you?' demanded the other. He was his insouciant self and he stood in an attitude of careless ease which might have deceived any man but Winter, who knew that the thumb hooked into the pocket of those baggy breeches touched a long-bladed knife and that Tony would strike long before the bigger man could drop his hand to his pistol pocket.

Winter forced a grin.

'Well, be cheerful if you feel like it,' he said. 'There's no reason, I can tell you.'

'What did the captain say?' asked Mrs Markham.

'What do you think he said?' growled the other. 'He made me feel a fool. You've got everything, Tony?'

The Spaniard nodded.

'The dog collar?'

The Spaniard nodded again.

'When did you give him that?' asked Winter suspiciously.

'Oh, yesterday,' said the woman.

Winter looked from one to the other suspiciously.

'That's a lie,' he said. 'Where is that collar?'

He made a step toward the deck.

'You can save yourself the trouble,' said Stella Markham coolly; 'the collar has been removed to a safe place.'

His heavy face was puckered and lined with fury, and he came back at her with a rush. Before he could lay his hand upon her or before Tony could slip between them there was a timid knock at the door.

'Who is that?' asked Winter.

Mrs Markham had stepped softly to the door, but he pushed her aside and pulled it open. Cecile Cameron was standing there and their eyes met for a moment. The scowl went out of Winter's face and a sly smile dawned slowly.

'Come in, Mrs Cameron,' he said politely.

She had no eyes but for Stella and went straight to the girl.

'Well?' it was Winter who spoke. 'What are you going to do to get your sister out of trouble?'

Cecile turned in alarm.

'Is she in – danger?' she asked in a low voice, and he growled impatiently.

'We are all in danger, don't you realise that?'

'I will do my best,' said Cecile Cameron wearily.

'You'll have to do a pretty good best too,' said Winter brutally. 'You can't save your sister without making some effort to save her husband.'

She met his eyes without flinching.

'I think I can do something,' she said. 'There is no charge against her and she has no existence to the detectives on board.'

'How do you know?' asked the man quickly.

Tony a silent spectator, smiled.

'She has interviewed the excellent Bartholomew,' he said, 'and what she tells us is a confirmation of my best hopes.'

'Your hopes?' Winter swung round on him.

'My hopes,' said the other. 'I desire most earnestly that madame should not appear in this matter if there is any question of police.'

John Winter was peering at him.

'So that's it, is it,' he said softly. 'That's the meaning of your sister's meetings, her visits night after night, and you said she was only trying to induce you to give up this kind of life! You were lying, eh? I suppose you've got it all framed up to put it on me, now Talbot's dead. And Tony's in it!'

'You're a fool!' said Tony quietly. 'I shall have to share whatever medicine they ladle out and I've got an idea it is going to be a stiff dose.'

Winter turned slowly to his wife. She was sitting with her head on her sister's shoulder and her eyes were closed. There was something pathetic in the weariness of the drawn face and the shadowed eyes, but Mr Winter was no sentimentalist.

'If you think you're going to get this scandal hushed up and that I'm going to be the goat who goes to jail whilst my dear wife is playing the society lady in England or New York, why you've got another guess coming,' he said, breathing heavily. 'You're in this with me, Stella, or Magda, or whatever your fool name is, and I'm ready to take the stand and prove you were in every job we did in Europe–'

'And I'm prepared to take the stand and prove that she was not,' said the little Spaniard.

'You!' snapped John Winter.

'Why not?' said Tony. 'I at least am as respectable as you!'

'All right.' John Winter turned to the door. Then suddenly the fury he had pent up and suppressed burst its bounds and with an oath he leapt at the white-faced girl, and his hand was at her throat when he felt a curious pain under the left shoulder, a sharp, hot twinge of agony that made him cry out and switch round.

'I gave you no more than a millimetre,' said Tony quietly and John Winter dropped his eyes to the long, thin blade in the Spaniard's hand. 'Only one millimetre! Imagine, my dear Winter, if I gave you seventy-five or eighty!'

Winter did not speak. He pulled open the door and blundered out, and when the women looked at Tony again his hands were empty and the knife had mysteriously disappeared.

16

'Here's the end of the road,' said Jim Bartholomew.

'Where?' The girl looked round startled.

A thin haze hung upon the sea, but the *Ceramia* was making her maximum speed.

'If you listen you will hear a hooter going in a minute. That's Fire Island and the United States.'

'You seem to know a lot about the voyage for one who has never been there,' she said.

'I've never been to the United States,' he confessed, 'but I have been to Fire Island Light. I came once on a cruise after a fugitive submarine in the bad old days.'

The siren of the lightship was now audible. They were standing on the foredeck beneath the captain's cabin and they heard the clang and grind of the telegraph and soon after the thud of the propellers came at longer intervals.

'We're slowing down,' he said.

'Listen.'

Margot took his arm in hers.

'Dear, I want to – ask you something.'

He knew what was coming and was silent.

'What is going to happen to Mrs Markham?' she asked, and he looked at her sharply.

'What do you know about Mrs Markham?' he demanded.

'Tell me what will happen to her.'

'Do you know who she is?'

She nodded.

'Cecile told me this morning,' she said. 'Mrs Markham is Cecile's sister – the one that was supposed to be dead, and she's married to that dreadful man whom she pretends is her butler.'

He looked thoughtfully over the side before he replied.

'Does Frank know?'

'Yes,' nodded the girl. 'She told Frank everything the day she was supposed to leave for Scotland. Frank has been a brick throughout. What is going to happen to Mrs Markham?' she asked again.

'Nothing,' said Jim. 'What poor Sanderson called the Big Four of Crime was never known under that title to the police either in England or in America. The people they have been after have been Talbot, Trenton, and Romano–'

187

She raised her eyebrows.

'Romano? You don't mean our beautiful little cavalry officer?'

'That is the gentleman,' said Jim grimly. 'But the name of Mrs Trenton has never appeared in any of the warrants. She was looked upon by Scotland Yard as being more or less of a victim, and I discovered from the conversation I had with the detectives that that is the view which the American police are taking. To make doubly sure one of them put through a code inquiry to Washington yesterday morning and had a reply which is quite satisfactory from Mrs Trenton's point of view. The only danger of course,' he said thoughtfully, 'is that Trenton, out of sheer malice, endeavours to drag Mrs – his wife down with him. The man is a fiend.'

Margot shivered.

'Isn't it dreadful to think about? She ran away with him, when she was at school – poor woman, she has been punished for her folly.'

'I hope her punishment is ended,' said Jim, and there was a great deal more in his speech than the girl could guess.

Winter had gone back to his wife's cabin and was packing when the telegraph had rung the engines to half-speed.

'Why are they slowing?' Stella asked listlessly.

'Why the hell don't you go and ask the captain?' snarled the other.

Mrs Markham shrugged.

'Really Winter, you grow more and more impossible. Throughout this voyage I have been trying to make things right for you and you've been trying to make them just as wrong as they can be.'

'When I want your advice I'll ask you for it,' he said. 'And when I want you to talk, why, I'll send you along a permit. At present you can close your mouth and sit tight. I've got something to settle with you – and Tony.'

He was busy strapping some bags and trunks. Mrs Markham sat with folded hands staring into vacancy.

'Whatever side of the Atlantic we live,' she said, 'there's hell and a worse hell in between.'

'Will you shut up?' he snarled, and lifted a hand threateningly. 'One of these days' – he glowered at her – 'one of these days, my lady–'

She shrugged her shoulders.

'One of these days I suppose I shall go the way of Talbot, and the way you tried to send

Jim Bartholomew.'

He walked to the window of her sleeping cabin and looked out. The swaying mast of a little boat was disappearing aft and his face went a dirty white.

'That's a police boat,' he said thickly.

She shrugged again and walked out of the room.

'Where are you going?'

'On to the deck to look.'

'Come back,' he shouted, and when she did not obey a suspicion of what was behind her action came to him and with a bellow of rage he ran after her.

He flew down the alleyway out on to the deck looking round for her. He did not see his wife, but he saw something else which made his blood turn cold.

Tony stood half a dozen paces from the saloon entrance and he was the centre of a group of three men, strangers who had evidently come aboard from the police boat, the mast of which showed above the rail, and though Tony was smiling and obviously conversational, the hand of one of the detectives which gripped the Spaniard's arm was self-explanatory.

He turned in a flash to go back the way he had come, but a fourth stranger was standing in the narrow doorway and behind him was Jim Bartholomew.

'You're wanted, Trenton,' said the man. 'And if you're sensible, you are not going to give me any trouble. Put out your hands.'

The game was up. Escape was impossible, and Trenton, his flabby face grey and old, held out his hands and the handcuffs were snapped on. The stranger gripped him by the arm and led him across to the group of which Tony Romano was the centre, and in that short space of time, Mr Winter, or John Winter Trenton, made up his mind.

'Good morning, chief,' he said, recognising one of Tony's captors.

'Good morning, Trenton,' he said coolly. 'The other man is dead, you say?' He spoke to the Scotland Yard detective at his side, but Romano answered.

'Yes, quite dead,' he said cheerfully. 'In fact, that I can certify because I killed him. Now, my dear Winter' – he smiled upon his companion – 'let us proceed.'

'Wait a moment,' said Trenton hoarsely. 'You want three of us, don't you?'

'Two alive and one dead,' said the police officer.

'Well, you're going to take three alive.'

They had not put the irons upon Tony

Romano and he was standing in his usual attitude of ease, a half smile on his thin, swarthy face.

'My friend,' he interrupted, 'you have heard the chief tell you that he requires three, two alive and one dead. Would you desire anything more than that?'

'Yes I would,' snarled Trenton.

'You are contemptible,' said Tony, 'but you shall have it different since you wish.'

He spoke so calmly and gave so little warning of his intentions that even the officer who held him was taken off his guard. He seemed to contract the muscles of the arm which was in his captor's grip and to leap forward at the same time, and those who watched thought he did no more than clumsily embrace his companion in misfortune, for he threw his arms around him.

'That will do!' said the chief sharply. 'Take that man, Riley.'

Then he saw Trenton's face, the chin resting on the Spaniard's shoulder, and in that face was a grimace of terror.

'Yes, that will do, I think,' said Romano, and as he disengaged himself from the other Trenton crumpled in a heap to the ground.

'And that, gentlemen, is the knife,' said the Spaniard pleasantly, dropping the long steel weapon to the deck.

Whilst they handcuffed him he was very talkative.

'You need not bother about Trenton,' he said. They were leaning over the prostrate man trying to staunch the wound in his back. 'He is quite dead, I assure you. In that same way did my friend Talbot die. It is better so. I do not like the idea of sharing a trial with such a man.'

They hurried him below to F Deck, where they made a quick but thorough search.

'I think you will find most of the jewels these people are bringing back in friend Romano's baggy breeches,' said Jim quietly.

Romano smiled.

'Otherwise, why the baggy breeches?' he said coolly. 'It is perfectly true, chief, and these garments,' he patted his pantaloons proudly with his cuffed hand, 'these garments are worth three million dollars.'

From an open port on F Deck a gangway led to the police boat. As they were taking him away Romano turned to Jim.

'My respectful salutations to all who have been kind to me,' he said. He looked the other straight in the eye and Jim knew that the message was for Stella Markham.

'Will you also apologise to Miss Cameron?

I went to her room to gain peace of mind. There was something there that I hoped to find. I was successful – it is there still.'

17

So they took away Tony Romano and carried with them also the bodies of the two men, and the passengers of the *Ceramia* heard for the first time of the tragedy which had occurred without their knowledge.

Then Jim sought the woman. She was not alone. Cecile was with her, her arms about her.

'Do they want me?' asked Stella Markham dully

Jim shook his head. He hesitated to tell of the Spaniard's deed by which he had forfeited what little chance he had had of escaping the Chair.

'I haven't had to explain your presence on the ship, Mrs Trenton,' he said. 'The only man who can betray you is dead.'

She nodded.

'Tony... Tony did that for me?'

It was not until that evening when they were gathered in Cecile's sitting-room at the hotel that she told her story.

'I ran away from school with my – husband. He was much older than I, and I suppose that I was fascinated – I was certainly a fool. He was not of the same social grade as my own people, but his lack of breeding might have been excused and he might, with his intelligence, have climbed very high indeed. But John Winter Trenton was always a crook, a crook in heart and a crook in mind. It was a long time before I learnt the truth, and when I did I suppose I wasn't as horrified as I should have been. At any rate, he could put things so attractively – I'm excusing myself,' she said, with a shrug. 'I went with him. I took a passive part in some of his most nefarious swindles and he got away with it for a long time. Then a clever woman detective got after us–'

Jim smiled.

'Why do you smile?'

'Curiously enough,' he said. 'I thought you were that woman detective when I began to get a glimmering of this story.'

Stella shook her head again.

'No, she has never left America. She had us arrested, Winter and I, and it was while we were waiting trial that I let my sister know what had become of me. For years Winter had been working a small game and then he got into a better set, mainly through the help of Talbot, and we came to Europe and they started the series of robberies which you know about. It was Winter who planned it all, Tony and Talbot who carried the plan into execution. I had nothing to do but pose as a grand lady. We rented expensive furnished houses, sometimes in the north of England, sometimes in the south, and from there the gang spread their nets. Winter, of course, posed as my butler.' She smiled faintly. 'There is a certain amount of humour in that. It was I who was that man's slave. He's dead,' she cried passionately. 'I'm glad he's dead! If I could thrust him down into hell with these hands...' She stood trembling in her passion, and then of a sudden broke into a fit of weeping.

'I think we know all there is to be known, Mrs Cameron,' said Jim. 'Does your husband know?'

'I told him,' said Cecile.

Jim went out of the room, taking Margot with him.

They were walking to the elevator when the girl asked:

'Why did you search her stateroom, Jim? Of course, you were the mysterious sailor whom she saw disappearing through the window? Did you expect to find anything?'

'I expected to find two things,' he said. 'I found one – the second ring, the Daughters of the Night. You remember Cecile telling us that her father had given both his girls a similar ring? That I found on my second visit. The other thing I sought I have never found and my failure is the bitterest disappointment to me. Do you know we have not recovered the jewels which were deposited by Mrs Markham and which probably today are her only assets, even though they were stolen! Incidentally we are responsible at the bank to the extent of £112,000. Here is the ring.'

He took it from his waistcoat pocket and showed it her. It was a replica of the ring which Mrs Cameron had worn, and the girl took it in her hands and admired it.

'It was the photograph of Mrs Markham wearing this ring, which poor Sanderson had. He must have caught a glimpse of her, and, utterly deceived by Winter's pleasant appearance, he invited Winter down the night Mrs Markham left Moorford, intending to employ, as he thought, an honest servant to pursue inquiries. I think he suspected Stella from what he had seen of her and her resemblance to the photograph, and he had arranged to interview Winter in order to get him to identify the police photo-graph of Mrs Trenton with the man's employer. I think that theory is as near correct as possible. It is impossible to get the correct one. Both the parties to that meeting are now dead.'

'What happened then?'

'Winter came to the bank that night. Mrs Markham may have been in the car – as to that I have no information. He was probably horrified to see the photograph, for if Stella was identified so was he. In desperation he must have threatened Sanderson, who produced my revolver. There was a struggle, that is clear from an overturned chair. Winter, who was a powerful man, must have secured possession of the revolver, shot Sanderson and torn the photograph from his hand, making his escape down the passage when I came through the door of my office.'

'But the jewels? What happened then?'

'I'll tell you what happened then,' said Jim. 'As I stood looking down at Sanderson I had an instinctive feeling that Mrs Markham was in some way mixed up in this case. I took my keys and opened the safe expecting to find Mrs Markham's packet gone. Sanderson had told me in the morning that Winter had been down to the bank looking at the package and sticking a label on it, and he also told me that Winter had drawn his attention to a man outside the window of the office whom he said his mistress did not like. I found the package and brought it to the table and, without any excuse from the strict point of view of a banker and a custodian, I broke the seals and opened the package, only to find, as I expected, the glass box was empty.'

'What had happened?' asked the girl.

'Winter had performed the very simple trick of 'ringing the changes.' He had brought with him to the bank that morning a package similarly sealed, and whilst he had drawn Sanderson's attention away by directing his eyes to somebody outside the window, he substituted the empty package for the other. As soon as I discovered the glass box was empty I knew that Winter was in it and just how Sanderson had been tricked. Mrs Markham I thought had already left. Probably Winter was on his way to Southampton with her. I had to think quickly. I took £200 out of my private drawer, raced home, took my bag which was already packed for my visit to London – I intended spending Sunday night in London – and caught the last train to Exeter. The rest of the story you know.'

'What did you expect to find on board the ship?'

He laughed.

'I expected to find the murderer. I was certain of finding you,' he said.

'And this man speaks of the two things both in the same breath,' said the girl wonderingly, 'and he expects me to go on loving him and cherishing him–'

'I know you will,' said Jim, 'because I tell you honestly the only thing that has spurred me on, the only thing that has kept my mind clear and my heart cheerful, has been the knowledge that you were near me.'

She looked at him, a keen, scrutinising glance. Three times the elevator door had opened, but the sorrowful 'Going down!' of the attendant had been unheeded.

'Do you mean that?'

'Of course I mean it,' he said indignantly.

'That's rather wonderful,' she said softly; and then, 'but you haven't told me what you did find. What has become of the necklace?'

He spread out his hands in despair.

'Tony's baggy riding breeches yielded enough stuff to keep a respectable jeweller going for ten years,' he said, 'but amongst those relics there was nothing that bore the remotest resemblance to Mrs Markham's dog collar, and that,' he said soberly, 'adds rather a gloom to the proceedings. Now I wonder–'

'Poor Mrs Markham! Poor Cecile! What will be the end of that?'

'The Lord knows!' he said.

'By the way, I wonder who her friend is in New York, the girl to whom I was to give the candies?'

'What friend in New York?' asked Jim, with sudden interest.

'Oh, some girl who will call for a box of–'

Jim gripped her with a yell.

'Where's that box?' he said, and her mouth opened wide.

'You don't mean–'

'Let me look at it.'

They flew down the corridor together and, defiant of all proprieties, Jim followed the girl into her room. She unlocked and opened her trunk and with trembling fingers tore the wrappings from the candy box.

Jim knocked the lid off and their faces fell.

'It is candy,' said Jim, 'unless–' He poked his finger down, then suddenly swept the chocolates aside and drew forth something which glittered even through the silver tissue in which it had been wrapped.

'Darling,' he said, 'this settles our future.'

'Our future was settled when you were rescued from a watery grave.'

Suddenly he whistled.

'Tony went to your stateroom?'

'The Italian – yes?' she said in surprise. 'I accused him – why?'

'He went to make sure that the box was there. The diamonds are Stella Markham's own property and he was worried about their disposal. He must have suspected that Stella had put them in your keeping, and searched your cabin "for his peace of mind" – those were his words. He loved her.'

'Loved her?' repeated Margot incredulously.

'He loved her and rescued her as assuredly as you rescued me, when you dived in your petticoat–'

She looked at him with a stern eye.

'You were supposed to be unconscious, Mr Jim Bartholomew.'

'And do you wonder?' demanded Jim.

The publishers hope that this book has given you enjoyable reading. Large Print Books are especially designed to be as easy to see and hold as possible. If you wish a complete list of our books please ask at your local library or write directly to:

Dales Large Print Books
Magna House, Long Preston,
Skipton, North Yorkshire.
BD23 4ND